GUARDIANS
of GA'HOOLE

Lost Tales of Ga'Hoole

OTULISSA

Editor in Chief

GUARDIANS
of GA'HOOLE

Lost Tales of Ga'Hoole

BY OTULISSA,
HISTORIAN OF THE GREAT TREE

With the Most Essential Guidance of Kathryn Huang

SCHOLASTIC INC.

New York Toronto London Auckland
Sydney Mexico City New Delhi Hong Kong

ISBN 978-0-545-10244-5

Design by Steve Scott

Illustrated by Richard Cowdrey

12 11 10 9 8 7 6 5 4 3 2   10 11 12 13 14 15/0

Printed in the U.S.A.   40

First printing, May 2010

Contents

GUARDIANS
of GA'HOOLE

Lost Tales of Ga'Hoole

Foreword

Greetings, Dear Readers!

I come to you not as a monarch, but as an old friend from the Great Ga'Hoole Tree. I write at Otulissa's request. She asks that I give you news of the tree and introduce the tales she has gathered. And so I shall.

It seems we have entered a time of blessed peace. The Striga and his vicious Blue Brigade fell in defeat many moon cycles ago. Nyra and the Pure Ones are gone. The dedication to learning fostered at the great tree has spread throughout the kingdoms, bringing with it the fresh breeze of knowledge and banishing the dank residue of ignorance, superstition, and malice. The arts of reading and even writing are no longer rare beyond the tree. Deep in the forest of Ambala, a simple printing press has been built with the help of the newly established research-and-printing chaw from the great tree, so that in that hidden dell where great works are chanted into the emerald air, they are now put down in printed scrolls and books as well. This new press, and our own press at the great tree, supply a small but growing number of lending libraries that have been established in the owl kingdoms, so that great works from the tree, from the Glauxian Brothers' and Glauxian Sisters' retreats, and from the library of the Others in the Palace of Mists, may be studied in distant dens and hollows by furred, scaled, and feathered scholars alike.

It is perhaps natural that in such times of outward peace, we look inward. And so it is that the personal and, in some cases, secret histories of our own Guardians and others close to the tree have now come to light. Otulissa has studied, researched, and sometimes simply listened with a wise and sympathetic ear slit, and set down the tales for all to learn from. As you read these tales of personal history, private anguish, and worldly adventure, remember that not all battles are fought in the air or on the ground. Some, perhaps the most difficult of all, are fought in our own gizzards, hearts, and brains.

I submit these tales to you with respect and affection.

Soren

Guardian Among Guardians

ONE

The Snowy Sisters

I think you all know of the Rogue smith of Silverveil and her sister, our very own Madame Plonk, the official singer at the great tree. Their contributions to the Southern Kingdoms and the great tree have been significant and many. But how well do we really know them? Many of you will just now be discovering that Madame Plonk's given name is Brunwella, and that the Rogue smith of Silverveil was once a young Snowy known as Thora. They each had a past that was full of drama, romance, treachery, and, of course, sisterly love.

In the early days of the Band, shortly before Soren, Gylfie, Digger, and Twilight became full-fledged Guardians, the Rogue smith of Silverveil made a shocking revelation to them without much explanation. After Madame Plonk lost her sister to the villainy of Nyra, she was utterly heartbroken, and said not a word for nights on end. When she finally spoke again, she told the tale behind her sister's startling confession.

Thora Plonk glided over the icy eastern coast of the Everwinter Sea. For the first time in days, her gizzard was relaxed. She had just spent much of the evening with her friend Sig. *No*, Thora reflected, *Sig was more than a friend*, and the thought made her almost giddy. She had just given him one of the first pairs of battle claws that she had ever made. It was a special gift, one that she wouldn't have given to just a friend. But as she neared the hollow that she shared with her da, stepmother, and sister, Thora's gizzard began to tighten. It was a familiar feeling, one that had plagued her ever since her return home after more than a year away from the family hollow.

Thora had been scarcely older than a fledgling when she fled her home. She and her sister, Brunwella, had lost their mum in the Battle of the Ice Talons — the final bloody battle of the War of the Ice Claws — less than a year earlier. Their da, an aging Snowy named Berrick, had taken their stepmother, Rodmilla, as a mate. Brunwella was so young when their mum died that she barely remembered her at all, but Thora remembered her vividly and missed her terribly.

Berrick had thought it important to find a new mate right away. When he met Rodmilla, he was completely besotted. She was fair, to be sure. But more important, she was completely different from his first mate, Thea, whose warring ways had left him mateless. Where Thea had gadfeather roots, Rodmilla came from an old and distinguished N'yrthghar clan; where Thea had been a fierce fighter with the Kielian League, the losers in the war, Rodmilla barely seemed to care about the war; where Thea spent night after night away from their hollow discussing war strategies with other fighters, Rodmilla was home plumping nests, studying her own illustrious ancestry, or doting on Berrick, whenever he was there. Berrick must have thought that he had found the perfect new mother for his owlets.

He may have been half right, Thora thought ruefully. Rodmilla immediately took to Brunwella. It was hard not to — Brunwella was a beautiful little owlet, the prettier of the two sisters even at a very young age. She was affectionate and agreeable. On top of it all, Brunwella had inherited the classic Plonk singing voice, with the promise of becoming the best singer of her generation. Thora, on the other wing, was no great beauty. True, she had lovely eyes and a quick wit, but she had suffered from a bad case of gray scale as an owlet and it had left her feathers dull and blotchy. She was also strong-willed and outspoken. When Rodmilla first moved into the hollow, she insisted that the sisters call her "Mother."

Brunwella had no trouble with this. After all, Rodmilla was the only mother she had ever known. But Thora resisted emphatically, muttering under her breath, "*That owl is not my mum.*" Rodmilla took this as a cue to be extra strict with the older sister.

The more Rodmilla tried to assert her authority, the more Thora resisted. Rodmilla's strictness verged on cruelty. She ignored Thora unless it was to tell her to do chores. When food was scarce in the depth of winter, and Berrick was away, Rodmilla fed Thora scraps and leftovers. Worst of all, Rodmilla openly called Thora "Splotch" because of the patchy coloration left by the gray scale.

Thora felt like an outcast in her own home, and she couldn't stand it. As soon as she summoned enough courage, she fled the hollow, bidding Brunwella a tearful farewell. For almost a year Thora flew about the Northern Kingdoms without a nest to call her own. Then she met a Kielian snake named Octavia, who told her about blacksmithing. One thing led to another, and Octavia introduced Thora to a Rogue smith on the island of Dark Fowl. His skill was legendary, and Thora became his apprentice.

Thora had a real talent for blacksmithing, learning quickly and easily. After a few short moon cycles, she began to forge battle claws — a task usually reserved for experienced smiths. Even though Dark Fowl was a desolate place constantly lashed by gales and ice storms, it felt more comfortable to Thora than her hollow in the Firth of Canis after Rodmilla moved in. And she suspected that her da knew where she had ended up. She was certain she spotted him more than once on Dark Fowl, watching over her from a distance, making sure she was all right. Despite missing him and her sister, she felt she belonged on Dark Fowl and had found her life's work in blacksmithing.

But Thora's happiness was short-lived. Her work as an apprentice took her all over Dark Fowl, and she'd learned that the grog trees, where Rogue smiths often gathered, were wonderful places to learn of the newest smithing techniques as the tipsy Rogue smiths boasted to one another. Then one day, she overheard a dark rumor concerning her own family. So alarming was this rumor that Thora feared for the safety of her da and sister back home. If it was true, then Berrick and Brunwella were in danger. Worry ate at Thora's gizzard. She had little choice — she had to go home to find out the truth. So, Thora made the difficult return to the home she hated.

Thora had braced her gizzard for a long stay. If the rumor proved false, then merely bringing it up would be hurtful to her family. And if it was true, she'd have to be careful — very careful. She had returned three moon cycles ago, and was still biding her time. Since her return, she had tried to act the remorseful runaway ready to become the dutiful daughter. She tried her best to make peace with Rodmilla, and it seemed that Rodmilla was doing the same. Even so, Thora was uncomfortable around her stepmother; she couldn't help it. But at least she was able to see her da and Brunie again. She had missed them terribly while she was away.

It was almost dawn. As she banked toward home, Thora thought about how excited Brunwella would be to hear all about her meeting with Sig tonight. That made her feel a little better.

Brunwella Plonk sat quietly in her nest. She was thinking about her da, Berrick. He was a healer, had been since the war. These days, he was often away from the hollow. She wished she could see more of him. She and her sister were near mating age and soon it would be time to leave the nest for good. She wondered what her da was doing right then. Collecting herbs, no doubt, and maybe making a poultice for some poor injured owl. Brunwella guessed that her father now and again even helped to heal wounded soldiers from the Resistance, but she and her sister never talked about it openly. To do so would be dangerous. Sympathizing with the defeated Kielian League was one thing; assisting the Resistance was quite another. It was considered an act of treason against the victors. Whatever her da was doing, Brunwella was certain it was very noble. She was so lost in her thoughts that she didn't even hear as her stepmum approached the hollow.

"HA! She's dead!"

And with that, Rodmilla Plonk, Brunwella and Thora's stepmother, broke the peace as she flapped into the hollow. She had been out with friends, and had clearly brought back a juicy bit of gossip.

"Old Melvonia Plonk has finally sung her last little ditty," she continued. "Oh, darlings, did you hear me? Melvonia is dead! The singer at the Great Ga'Hoole Tree is DEAD!"

The very pitch in which Rodmilla squawked, which is to say, so high that it was beyond the hearing range of some older owls, could only mean that she was extremely excited. Melvonia was known in the Northern and Southern Kingdoms alike simply as Madame Plonk, the esteemed singer of the Great Ga'Hoole Tree — the chosen one of her generation. And the death of the great tree's singer was big news indeed, for a new singer would have to be chosen.

"Mother, I wish you'd show some sympathy," Brunwella said. She, too, had heard of the news earlier that night. "I heard she died suddenly, and she was so young. I think it's quite sad."

"Oh, shush up, Brunwella. What do you know? Where's your sister? She needs to hear this! Thora? THOOOR-RAH!" With that, Rodmilla flew out of the hollow that she shared with her mate and her two step-daughters.

Odd . . . Brunwella thought; Thora wouldn't care one bit about the death of Melvonia, the singer of the Great Ga'Hoole Tree. Why was Rodmilla so intent on telling her? If anything, Brunwella would be the one most affected by the news. She had long been considered a very talented singer of her generation and had been primed nearly since hatching to sing at the voice trials that would decide the next singer.

"Where has that stubborn owl gone off to?" Rodmilla screeched when she failed to find Thora.

"I haven't a clue, Mother," Brunwella answered, although she was almost certain that Thora was off with Sigfried again. And Sigfried, bless his gizzard, was exactly "the wrong sort of Snowy" according to her stepmother. "She's probably just out hunting," Brunwella added casually, trying to cover her little lie.

"Hunting? Well, that's the last thing she should be doing. That girl needs to cut back on those plump little snow mice this time of year — and attend to her figure!" Rodmilla stopped fretting for a second and eyed her younger daughter up and down. "You ought to think about cutting back, too, dear."

There it was again: "cutting back." Both Brunwella and Thora were awfully thin. It was a harsh winter and food was scarce. Brunwella knew that "cutting back" was her stepmother's subtle way of reminding her and her sister that it was time for the two of them to leave the nest. When Thora had left the first time, Brunwella could tell that her stepmother was secretly pleased, though when she came back, Rodmilla had acted overjoyed.

"Oh, I do wish that girl would just stay where I can find her," Rodmilla continued to fret.

Brunwella rolled her yellow eyes. *Mother sure is fired up today.* When the moon had started newing, they had gotten word that they would be receiving a special visitor come full moon — a visitor by the name of Henryk, Marquis Henryk VI, to be exact. Although most owls in the Northern Kingdoms had done away with such titles ages ago — they were next to meaningless, after all — some families still clung to them. Generation after generation, they prided themselves on being direct descendants of one royal or another. "Why, he's the catch of the firths! And he'll be staying in Firth of Canis for a full moon cycle!" Rodmilla had screeched when she first learned of the visit. The sisters were familiar with Rodmilla's obsession with her own semi-noble heritage and her apparent desire to climb ever higher on the social thermals.

As dawn neared, Thora returned, breathing hard after having flown fast and far.

"Where have you been? Mother has been desperately trying to find you," Brunwella whispered to her sister as she met her just outside their hollow. "I can only cover for you for so long."

"With Sig," Thora whispered giddily.

"Are you two courting?" Brunwella whispered back excitedly. She noticed, then, that her sister's feathers were covered in soot. "And why are you all dirty?"

Thora lowered her head sheepishly. "I wouldn't call it courting exactly. . . . Sig took me to meet some of his friends. And I got my talons on the forge last night. I've missed it so terribly since my return to this Glaux-forsaken hollow, Brunwella! I can't wait to go back."

Imagine, my own sister, a blacksmith. It was just like Thora — always the nonconformist. "Well, you'd better dust yourself off and go find Mother."

"Why? What's happened?"

"We got news that Madame Plonk just died," Brunwella answered.

"Is that all? What does that have to do with me?" Thora asked.

"I don't know. You know how she gets." Brunwella didn't know why Rodmilla had been looking for Thora. She couldn't help but think Rodmilla was acting strangely lately. For one thing, Thora wasn't the best singer in the family; that was certainly Brunwella. Thora had a good singing voice, better even than most Plonks. Still, anyone with ear slits had to admit that her tone was not nearly as good as Brunwella's. Where Thora's tone was strong like iron, Brunwella's shimmered like gold. Furthermore, Thora didn't care one bit for singing. It was Brunwella who was born with the gadfeather spirit.

For as long as there had been a Great Ga'Hoole Tree, a Snowy Owl from the Plonk family, all direct descendants of the Snow Rose, has tolled the passage of time there as its official singer — simply known as Madame or Sir Plonk. The most talented singer in each Plonk generation was chosen, and it was considered a great honor. When a singer died, a young owl from the next generation who had yet to mate was chosen by the heads of the Plonk clan to go to the tree. Brunwella had always dreamed that she might one day become that singer.

"Oh, there you are, Thora," Rodmilla said in an exasperated tone. "I've been looking all over for you."

"I was just, um . . . out . . ." Thora began to explain.

"I don't care where you've been. But now that you're back, we must begin your voice lessons."

"Voice lessons? Mother, do you have me confused with Brunie or some other owl?" Thora said with a sarcastic churr.

"Don't be fresh, Thora! Come, come, we must prepare and there's not much time; we have to increase your range, improve your breathing, and perfect your vibrato. All that can be taught, you know. How else are you going to be chosen to be the next Madame Plonk?"

"Madame Plonk?!" both Thora and Brunwella said in unison, thoroughly confused. Brunwella was the one who ought to be going to the voice tryouts, and she thought she had a good shot, too.

"Mother, you know full well that Brunwella is the one with the voice. Shouldn't she be the one to go to the voice trials?" Thora tried to reason.

"I have other plans for Brunwella. Now, let's begin with some scales."

"What plans?" Brunwella asked. *This doesn't sound good,* she thought.

"I'll have no more questions from you two tonight. Now. Thora. Scales."

Thora and Brunwella shot each other a suspicious look. They would have to discuss this in private tomorrow. The sun was already on the horizon, and Rodmilla was still insisting that Thora carry on with this rehearsal. Brunwella listened as her sister begrudgingly sang the scales. All Snowies in the Plonk family sang. It was simply a way of life. Tonight, however, Thora's voice sounded tired and weak. Rodmilla pushed on.

"Be careful, dear, watch the area between your chest register and head voice!" Rodmilla reminded her.

"I'd rather be watching the area behind my eyelids, Mother."

"Shush up with the talking! No talking, I only want to hear the scales. Start again with F. Loose and open throat. And . . ."

Why must she make such a chore of singing? Brunwella thought. She loved to sing. Whenever she was alone or off hunting with Thora, she could barely stop herself from singing. It was just so uplifting, so freeing. This practice Thora was being subjected to was exactly the opposite. By the time Thora had gotten to scales in the key of A, Brunwella had drifted off to sleep.

As focused as Rodmilla appeared to be on Thora's singing, her mind and her gizzard were straying toward other things. Rodmilla was determined to send the oldest of her stepdaughters to the great tree. *What a perfect way to get that one out of the hollow — in fact, out of the Northern Kingdoms.* That would solve half of her problems! Who would have thought that her plans would come together so quickly? Just when she was ready to go to extremes to get rid of Thora, the current Madame Plonk goes and drops dead. She must be careful now; this was *big*.

The next evening, before the sun had a chance to set, Thora and Brunwella woke up to their stepmother dusting under their nests.

"Time to wake up, dears!" Rodmilla said cheerfully. She nearly dumped Brunwella out of her nest. "Our honored guests arrive tomorrow. This awful little hole must be made perfect for Marquis Henryk VI and his lovely parents."

"Mother, I don't know why you're so concerned about impressing them," Brunwella complained in between yawns. "I've heard they're boring fuddy-duddies, not to mention complete Snow snobs." "Snow snobs" was the nickname given to Snowy Owls who only socialized with other Snowies. Of course, in the firths, where there were few owls of other species, it was not hard to be a Snow snob. Brunwella and Thora, however, made friends easily with owls of all species.

"They're *royalty*, my dear. Their bloodline goes back to the H'rathian court. They have very close ties to those in power. And since the defeat of the Kielian League" — she shot her stepdaughters a hard look — "they've become *very* important. While *this* family is one of commoners, descended from *gadfeathers*, for Glaux's sake. It's an honor that the marquis and his family would even deign see us. We have to work hard to impress them. How else do you think we're to get young Henryk to propose to you, hmm?"

"PROPOSE?!" Brunwella and Thora asked at once.

"Of course, dears! Oh, Brunwella, if we play this right, your chicks will have royal blood running through their veins." Rodmilla was giddy, so giddy that she didn't even notice that her younger stepdaughter was on the verge of going yeep. "Now, girls, lend a talon, this lemming feast won't serve itself, you know."

Brunwella was aghast. She couldn't take a mate now,

much less one like Henryk. If she did, her chances of becoming the next singer would be ruined. Tradition at the great tree demanded the singer be unmated at initiation. And Thora, the singer at the great tree? Unlikely, indeed. Thora would rather forge iron into Glaux knows what! *Just what is going on here? Why is Mother so determined to get us out of the hollow?*

The next night, their guests arrived. Henryk's parents, a plump pair of old owls whose spots had all but faded to a dull shade of gray, arrived first. Young Henryk flew into the hollow after them. He was small for a male Snowy, and Brunwella towered over him.

"Welcome! Welcome to our humble home!" Rodmilla trilled, bowing deeply with outspread wings. "I trust your flight wasn't too dreadful." She stuck out her talon and prodded Thora, urging her and Brunwella to bow as well.

"It was as dreadful as dreadful can be," grumbled Marquis Henryk V, father of young Henryk.

"Yes," the portly marquise said, "my poor mate was just tossed around by these awful winds. It's a good thing he's such a strong flier, even at his age."

"Oh, my dear Marquise Gertrude," Rodmilla frothed, "I do apologize for the weather here, it *is* dreadful. So good of all of you to make the trip." Rodmilla bowed again, so deep this time, she almost tumbled forward, head over tail.

Thora was disgusted at her mother's desperate attempts to charm the primaries off their guests. She clearly wanted Henryk to fall in love with Brunwella. That wouldn't be too hard, Thora figured. Brunwella's beauty and grace were well known in the firths. Henryk was not exactly a catch; he was neither attractive nor a genius. He would be doing very well for himself with Brunwella as his mate, despite her family's connection to the defeated Kielian League. But would Brunwella ever agree to such a thing?

"Well, the weather need no longer concern us," the old marquis piped up again. "Just point me in the direction of some strong bingle juice and I'll recover soon enough." He headed straight for the nut cups that had been set out, needing no direction from Rodmilla.

"And you must be Marquis Henryk VI. I'm honored, truly honored." She bowed once again to the younger marquis.

"Yes, a pleasure to meet you," Henryk said to Rodmilla, all the while not taking his eyes off Brunwella. "I assume these are your stepdaughters then?"

"Oh, yes, where are my manners?! Allow me to introduce you. This is Brunwella, the pride of the Firth of Canis, the one I wrote to you about. And this is . . . this is . . ."

"Thora, Mother. My name is Thora."

Rodmilla let out an embarrassed churr and gave her oldest a hard stare. "Yes, my other stepdaughter, Thora." Brunwella was sure she saw the young Henryk wince as he laid eyes upon Thora. It made her dislike him immediately.

"Brunwella," Rodmilla said, quickly diverting her guests' attention, "why don't *you* show Marquis Henryk to the refreshments."

Thora watched her stepmother's awkward social maneuvering. Whenever Rodmilla was nervous she had a habit of tucking her left leg behind her right to hide a missing talon lost in some accident long ago. She was doing it now. In fact she spent much of the evening with her left leg behind her right.

The lemming feast went off flawlessly, exactly as Rodmilla had planned it. Thora and Brunwella had hunted enough lemmings to feed a battalion the previous night — no easy feat these days. They counted: The young marquis ate five. Marquise Gertrude ate four. The elder marquis, however, only had an appetite for bingle juice, it seemed.

Young Henryk chatted with Brunwella all night. First, it was about his friends, or "school chums," as he called them. Then it was about his elite education: "Graduated from Featherston's Academy. Did you know you have to have connections just to be accepted?" And finally, he went on and on about his royal lineage, and how proud he was of the history of his family: "We can trace our roots back to the H'rathian court, you know. Very few Snowies can say that."

Brunwella was so bored she had to keep pinching her own leg with her talon to keep from nodding off. She and Thora exchanged exasperated looks, but even that got old as the night went on. Rodmilla, on the other hand, acted as if every word out of young Henryk's beak was fascinating. If Brunwella had to hear her stepmother gasp "You don't say!" one more time, she was going to yarp her lemming before it was fully digested. Thora was thrilled that she was largely ignored all night long.

When Rodmilla asked, or rather told, Brunwella to sing a song for their guests, she felt positively ill. She obliged, of course, and sang a traditional hymn called "Blessed Snow." She considered, just for a second, belting out an old gadfeather tune, just to see what would happen. But she knew Rodmilla would be furious and she didn't see the point of upsetting her. Besides, Thora seemed to think something more sinister was in the works, though what could be more sinister than selling your stepdaughter off to petit nobility for some paltry increase in your own social standing, Brunwella couldn't imagine.

As the blackest part of the night approached, the feast finally began to wind down. The elder Marquis Henryk, who was now barely coherent, raised his umpteenth nut cup of bingle juice and said, "Allow me to propose a toast! To our gracious hostesses: Rodmilla, whose bingle juice is delicious and whose stepdaughter is . . . I mean, whose stepdaughters are as lovely as she promised they would be."

"Oh, how charming. Thank you, I'm honored, truly," Rodmilla replied. "The bingle juice I can't take credit for, but I will say that I am quite proud of my stepdaughters. I knew I had something special the day I met little Brunwella. She was the most beautiful little white chick you have ever seen."

Thora had to stop herself from rolling her eyes. It was hard for her to believe that this foolish, fawning, portly Snowy, who was her stepmum, was capable of the deeds the rumor claimed. She would have to watch her — carefully.

Just then, young Henryk lifted his nut cup a little higher. "Well, then, allow *me* to propose a toast." He winked at Brunwella, none too subtly. "To more little white chicks!"

Thora burst out churring so hard that she almost fell off her perch. Thankfully, the guests took her to be a tad tipsy, and let out uncomfortable little churrs of their own. Rodmilla was, of course, infuriated, but she would never let that show in front of *these* guests.

Brunwella was hyperventilating. "I can't do it, Thora, I just can't! I'd rather die!"

Thora looked down and read the letter that had just dropped from her sister's talons. *He must have had a scribe do this*, was her first thought. She was surprised the young marquis could construct a coherent sentence, despite his education.

> *To my dearest Brunwella,*
>
> *I have not stopped thinking about you since you sang "Blessed Snow" all those nights ago. I trust that you have not stopped thinking about me, either. After careful consideration, I have decided that you would make a suitable mate for me. Your beauty has truly bewitched me. While it is against tradition for a Snowy Owl of my social status*

to court a plebeian such as yourself, I believe that can be
overlooked in your special case. I propose that we begin
our courtship flight as soon as possible.

Yours,

Marquis Henryk, the Sixth of His Name

"I can't possibly take this Snow snob as a mate. He makes me physically ill! I can't become a part of his awful family. And the voice tryouts at the great tree! What about them?"

Thora had never seen her sister like this. She had wilfed to nearly the size of a chick. But she had to admit she was relieved by Brunwella's reaction to the young marquis' proposal.

Brunwella continued. "Mother had the nerve to keep this letter from me! Can you believe it?"

Thora took a deep breath. "She has been acting suspiciously, hasn't she?" Then she added, "This whole thing with me and the voice tryouts is strange, too. I'm not sure where it's all going, but I know I don't like it. And frankly, I fear unwanted proposals are the least of it."

Thora's thoughts were growing darker, while her sister's thoughts ran on to her dreams of singing at the great tree.

"Well, we have to do something about it!" Brunwella said. "The voice tryouts are tomorrow and I plan to be there, whether she likes it or not. And this business?" Brunwella waved Henryk's letter. "No way is this going to happen!"

"You're right, Brunie. You should be the one to go to the tryouts. I'll simply refuse to sing, that's all. What can she do, force me? And let's see what Da has to say about this proposal. He would never let you marry an Ice Talon! I have a plan." Thora got serious. "I say we go find Da tomorrow, after the voice trials; he'll put an end to all this nonsense."

"How will we do that? We have no idea where he is," Brunwella argued.

"Actually, I do," Thora admitted sheepishly. "Oh, Brunie, I didn't want to keep it from you, but these things are always top secret . . . and I didn't want to worry you." Thora looked around to make sure they were completely alone. "Sigfried has just joined the Resistance. I've been meeting him in secret. The Resistance hideout is on Dark Fowl Island. He told me that Da has been visiting it almost every day. We are sure to find him there."

Brunwella was taken aback. She knew he sympathized

with the Resistance, but nothing as serious as this. *Da, living a secret life, and everybody knew but me!*

"Does Rodmilla suspect?" she asked.

"No, I don't think so," Thora answered. Then a grim thought clouded Thora's mind. "For glaumora's sake," she whispered, "let's hope not."

"All right," Brunwella said after she let it all sink in. "After the tryouts then, we'll go find Da."

The night of the voice tryouts would be the perfect time for their expedition. Rodmilla would be forbidden to accompany Thora into the cave where the tryouts were to take place — the singer must stand alone, no coach is allowed to be present. Brunwella would tell her stepmother that she would accompany Thora most of the way there, to help her with a little last-minute rehearsal. Then, unbeknownst to Rodmilla, Brunwella would be the one to sing at the trial. Afterward, she and Thora would fly due south together for Dark Fowl. They would be long gone before Rodmilla figured out anything was amiss.

Rodmilla had given Thora and her sister exact instructions about their behavior at the voice trials, but on the night of the tryouts, Rodmilla was nowhere to be found. *Just as well,* thought Brunwella. They flew without a word to the appointed place. Thora bid her sister good luck on a ledge outside the cave where the Plonk family selection committee had gathered for the occasion. She listened closely as Brunwella began singing an old gadfeather ballad that had been sung by Snowies in the Northern Kingdoms for generations. Her voice rang out with clarity and aching tenderness.

Brunwella could not have sung more beautifully that night. Tears welled in Thora's eyes as Brunwella finished it. As the sisters took off for Dark Fowl Island, Thora had no doubt that Brunwella would become the next Madame Plonk. She would find out later that the selection committee agreed.

The winds were rough and made for slow flying. As dawn threatened, Thora and Brunwella were dismayed to realize that they had only gotten as far as the Bay of Fangs, just off the H'rathghar glacier. Lighting down wasn't a part of their plan, but they realized they would be forced to. There was no way they could reach Dark Fowl before first light at this rate. As they circled the bay, looking for a ledge or a cave to spend the day in, they spotted an owl, a Whiskered Screech whose labored wing strokes could only mean that he was injured. The Whiskered Screech had spotted them, too, and cautiously flew a little closer to investigate.

"Who goes there?" he called out.

That raspy voice sounded awfully familiar to Thora. She banked a little a closer to get a better look. "Torsten?" she finally asked.

"Thora?" The owl recognized Thora right away.

"He's a friend of Sig's from the Resistance!" Thora told her sister. The three owls landed on a ledge in an ice wall. Brunwella was nervous. She'd never knowingly associated with anyone actually *in* the Resistance.

"Am I glad to see a friendly face!" Torsten was breathing heavily. His port wing had a small gash where it joined his shoulder. He seemed relieved to stop flying for the moment. "I have bad news, I'm afraid." His face turned grave as he steadied himself on the ledge.

"What happened?" Thora asked.

Torsten looked at Brunwella suspiciously. Thora suddenly realized that her sister was a stranger to this owl, and quickly made an introduction. "It's okay, this is my sister, Brunwella. You can trust her."

Torsten began his tale. "A small group of us raided the Ice Talons' headquarters at nightfall. We were desperate for supplies, and thought we could get in and out of their storage hollow without much trouble. Well, we were wrong. For some reason, they had the place on lockdown and had doubled the guards. We tried to abort the mission when we realized, but it was too late.

We took heavy casualties. I'm sorry to tell you this, Thora, but Sig was hurt, he was hurt bad."

Thora wilfed. Her beak dropped open but no words came out.

"Is he alive?" Brunwella finally asked the question that she knew Thora was trying to ask. "I mean, is he going to be okay?"

"I don't know," Torsten answered feebly. "We brought him back to Dark Fowl Island. There are Kielian snakes tending to him now, but he needs a healer. I was actually on my way to find your father."

"So were we."

The three owls had to think fast. It was Thora who came up with the new plan. Brunwella would accompany Torsten back north to find their father, Berrick, famed healer and, apparently, member of the Resistance. Torsten believed that he was back in the firths, finishing up a mission, so that was where they would go first. In the meantime, Thora would fly on to Dark Fowl to check on Sig. Then they would all meet back on Dark Fowl, hopefully with Berrick in tow.

"Right you are," Torsten said. "Berrick will know what to do. Caches of weapons, areas of Kielian loyalists, slipgizzles; he's got it all in his head."

Thora and Brunwella shot each other stunned looks.

Their father was no casual sympathizer treating the occasional wounded rebel. He wasn't just a fighter, either. He was an organizer, a high-ranking commander! Thora's gizzard soared. Their little expedition suddenly got a lot more interesting.

The sun had already edged over the horizon and painted the snowy landscape shades of orange and yellow, but Thora pushed on and arrived on Dark Fowl Island. She had been to this part of the island several times since Sig first introduced her to the Resistance, and found their hideout easily. What she saw inside the cave was devastating. Several owls were wounded, lying in make-shift nests and being tended to by a few Kielian snakes. Toward the right side of the cave, near the entrance, she found Sigfried.

"Sig?" She approached him. "It's Thora, I'm here." She saw the gash on his breast then. It had been covered with wet moss, but it still looked awfully painful.

He was badly hurt, but reached a wing out toward her. "Is it really you? I can't believe you came. There's something I need to tell you."

Before Sig could say more, Thora saw the battle claws beside his nest, well made and almost brand-new.

"You wore the battle claws I forged into a real battle?" Thora asked, surprised. The battle claws she had given to Sig were simple by battle claw standards, but they were perfectly balanced and meticulously made. She knew Sig thought highly of her special gift, but never thought he would wear them, much less into a real battle.

"The claws were effective, Thora. I took out three Ice Talon guards with them before . . ." Sig's voice trailed off and his face turned grim with pain.

"But listen now, this is important," Sig began again. "While I was at the Ice Talons' headquarters, I overheard two slipgizzles giving their reports in a cave near where the supplies are kept. One of the voices sounded awfully familiar, so I listened for a while. She kept talking about how she had finally managed to get the information from her 'target' and how 'circumstances' might force her to 'move faster with the operation' than she intended." Sig paused and took a deep breath. "Thora, I'm sorry to tell you this, but it was Rodmilla. Your stepmother is a slipgizzle for the Ice Talons."

"So it's true, the rumor was true all along," Thora murmured. "The worst of it. It's all true."

Brunwella and Torsten decided to look for Berrick at the family hollow first, or as Torsten put it: "Reconnoiter home base." Brunwella approached ahead of him. She was stunned by what she saw. In the one night that she and Thora had been gone, the hollow had been ransacked. There were papers strewn everywhere, every nest was turned upside down. A nut cup of ink had been knocked down and ink tracked over the scattered papers. Even the moss from the nests was thrown across the floor. Just beyond where her father's nest had been, she saw something that she had never noticed before — a small compartment hidden behind a stone.

"Brunwella!" came the familiar voice from the shadows just behind her in the hollow's entranceway.

"Da!" With a start, Brunwella turned to find her father in the hollow with Torsten at his side. Berrick swelled to almost twice his usual size upon finding what had happened to his family's home. He immediately looked over to the small, once-hidden compartment that Brunwella was just looking at and gave an angry hoot. Then he went over to the ink-smeared papers scattered on the floor and lowered his big head to study them. After a moment of silence a blood-curdling screech came from his beak. Torsten gave him a startled look.

"Da, what's happened?" Brunwella asked, still in shock.

"Look here, Brunie, and tell me what you see." He pointed down to the ink-marked papers.

She did as he said. "They are talon prints, Da."

"And is there anything strange about them?"

Brunwella looked at them again. "Yes. Here. On the left side, the last talon is missing . . . just like —"

"Just like your stepmother's. We have to leave this place immediately. As to the prints, suffice it to say, your mother is not who I thought she was. Let's go find your sister."

Brunwella had never seen her father act this way. He turned to Torsten: "Go to the hideout south of the Ice Fangs. Warn them that the Ice Talons know of their location. Now."

Torsten left the hollow and flew as well as his wounded wing could carry him. As Berrick and Brunwella took off, she tried to explain to her father what had happened in the last few nights. Berrick listened, and seemed to be thinking hard about what to tell his daughter. Finally, he spoke.

"Sometime ago I heard a rumor. An Ice Talon slip-gizzle had supposedly infiltrated the family of an old Kielian League soldier, and was working to take down the Resistance. Brunie, I told myself it was just a rumor. Forced it out of my mind. But I should have known. Her constant questioning, all the times she disappeared, supposedly to hunt but never brought back any food ... I should have known all along," his anguished voice began to trail off. "I am such an old fool."

Rodmilla and three Ice Talons guards approached Dark Fowl Island from the east. She wasn't happy about having to move faster than she had planned, but it would have to do. It was awfully bold of the Resistance to fly right into the heart of Ice Talons territory to attack a storage hollow, and after Rodmilla and her troops finished this short reconnaissance mission and reported back to headquarters, the rebels would suffer dearly for their daring: It was time for payback. She'd finally discovered the location of the Resistance's hideout — a quick search of the secret compartment behind Berrick's nest had given her that. To think, she had thought her mate was a dotard — an old fool looking for adventure, gathering herbs, tending to the occasional wounded rebel he chanced to stumble upon. No, her Berrick turned out to be much more than that! Who knew that the key maps and all the information she'd been searching for were right under her beak the entire time! The

Great Horned guard, who was flying point, signaled to Rodmilla and the others that it was time to make their descent.

Their mission was to scout out the rebel hideout in advance of an attack by a larger force. The four owls would approach the Resistance pretending to be locals wanting to join the Resistance. No one would recognize Rodmilla as an Ice Talon, after all, and the guards flying at her side were new recruits. The Ice Talons would return with a larger team later, after she gave them a report of the reconnaissance.

The plan was for Rodmilla to enter first and speak to whoever was in charge. She *had* always been the best sweet-talker in the Northern Kingdoms. But as soon as Rodmilla entered the cave of the rebel hideout, she knew her mission had fallen apart.

"Rodmilla!" Thora shouted. She had almost said "Mother" but that just felt wrong under the circumstances.

Rodmilla was only stunned for a moment. Then her voice turned venomous. "Well, well . . . Thora, fancy meeting you here, among the rebels!"

"Turnfeather! How dare you?"

"Oh, no, I'm not a turnfeather, dear. I have always been on the same side — the *winning* side. An Ice Talon

35

through and through. I should have known that you would join this sad little Resistance. You are your mother's daughter, after all. And I should have known that you would be the one to ruin all my hard work." Rodmilla eyed Sig, who was trying desperately to get up. "Is that your *intended*, then? I blame him, too. His little raid made against our storage hollow forced us to set things in motion earlier than I had wanted. It really is too bad for you lovebirds, and for your little sister and your pathetic father, too."

"Brunwella? And Da? What have you done to them?" Thora asked.

"Nothing . . . yet. I had it all figured out for both of you. I got Henryk to propose to our pretty little Brunwella, and I was about to accept on her behalf. It would have been quite an alliance. The marriage would have solidified the firths' allegiance to the Ice Talons, and your father would have had to make certain . . . concessions when it came to his involvement in the Resistance. And you, well, you were too ugly to marry off, but your voice isn't half bad, and I thought I could have gotten rid of you by sending you to the Southern Kingdoms to be a singer. I was going to get rid of both of you without hurting either of you, so don't blame me when it ends otherwise. You've gone and ruined it all. Whatever happens now, it's your fault!"

Rodmilla's eyes glowed a deadly yellow as she took to the air inside the small cave with battle claws extended. Thora stumbled back in shock, not knowing what to do. Rodmilla was almost on top of her.

"NO!" Sig screamed and threw himself in between Rodmilla and Thora.

There was a blur of gray and white feathers and the sound of metal tearing into flesh. The next thing Thora knew, Sig was lying in a heap on the cave floor, and Rodmilla was still advancing. Thora reached for the battle claws, the ones that she had made in Orf's forge. She had never flown with battle claws before, and had no idea how to use them, but they would be better than nothing. As she fumbled, she saw shapes out of the corner of her eye.

"Get away from my daughter!" It was Berrick, her father, and Brunwella was right behind him. "Brunie, stay back, out of the way," Berrick shouted.

Berrick charged at his mate with bare talons outstretched. "You treacherous . . ."

"Da!" Brunwella screamed before Berrick could finish the thought.

The Great Horned Owl who arrived with Rodmilla was in the cave and began slashing at Berrick. Bare-clawed, Berrick was no match for him. In a second, his wing was broken.

It was Rodmilla who delivered the death blow. "Good-bye, my gullible one," she whispered to her dying mate.

"Da, no!" Brunwella cried out.

As she heard her sister's cry, Thora lifted into the air, now with battle claws strapped firmly to her feet. She had never even fought before, much less fought to kill. But her gizzard took over. She didn't even have to think. She advanced toward her stepmother without hesitation. Rodmilla was the one on the defensive now, parrying Thora's blows. She was pinned against the cave wall as Thora's battle claws lashed out.

Rodmilla screeched in desperation, "Thora! Did I not try to spare you?"

As if in a trance, Thora said nothing. Her starboard claw drove deep into Rodmilla's throat, killing her.

By now, many Resistance fighters had come to the cave, and it was an all-out battle. The Great Horned turned his attention to fight alongside his two fellow Ice Talons guards, but the three of them were easily out-numbered and defeated.

In the end, all four Ice Talons, including Rodmilla, were killed. But they had taken with them the lives of the two owls most dear to Thora and Brunwella — Berrick and Sigfried were gone. The sisters collapsed into a heap and cried, holding each other in their wings. They remained in this sad embrace until the sun began to set.

The next night, Thora, Brunwella, and the owls of the Resistance burned Berrick's and Sig's bodies using coals from Orf's forge. As the fire burned, Brunwella began to sing.

> *Fly away with me.*
> *Give my loneliness a break.*
> *Fly away with me, so my heart will stop its ache.*
> *Rise into the night,*
> *Fly away with me.*
>
> *Fly with me till dawn,*
> *Hollows we shall leave behind.*
> *Fly with me till dawn, to places they'll never find.*
> *By the pale moonlight,*
> *Fly with me till dawn.*
>
> *Soar over this land,*
> *In the night sky we'll find glee.*

Soar over this land, see the steam rise from the sea.
Soft winds do invite,
Soar over this land.

Fly away with me,
My love, don't hesitate.
Fly away with me, for I can hardly wait.
Our hearts shall take flight,
Fly away with me.

It was the same song she had sung on the night of voice tryouts, which now seemed so long ago.

Thora listened to the old gadfeather words — "fly away" — and realized it was exactly what she and her sister needed to do. After the ceremony, she told Brunwella.

"Brunie, I think it's time we fly away from here."

"But where will we go?" Brunwella asked.

"South," Thora said definitively. "I don't think there is anything left for us here in the Northern Kingdoms. Sig told me that his family lives in a place called Silverveil. I want to go find them and tell them what happened here, that their son died a hero. Who knows, maybe they can use a Rogue smith. And you, I think you're sure to be chosen as the next singer at the great tree."

Brunwella was still hesitant. "It's such a long way away. . . ." But she thought about the lyrics she had just sung and grew brave. "You know what, you're right, Thora. Let's fly away."

The next night, a letter would arrive at the hollow once shared by Berrick, his mate Rodmilla, and his two daughters. It would confer the title of Singer at the Great Ga'Hoole Tree on Brunwella Plonk. But no one was there to receive it.

The two sisters flew south together in the moonlight, leaving behind their aching hearts in the frozen north. They flew on for many days, and then they went their separate ways — one to a life of seclusion and anonymity at a forge in the Forest of Silverveil, and the other to a life of fame and esteem at the great tree.

TWO

Fritha's Painted Past

As a ryb, I have had my share of bright students. A few of them rise above the rest. These are the young owls who make me feel truly blessed to be a ryb at the Great Ga'Hoole Tree. You may know one such student as the assistant editor of The Evening Hoot. Yes, I speak of none other than the Pygmy Owl Fritha. Fritha is clever, hardworking, diligent . . . well, I could go on and on. She came to the great tree in the time of the Great Flourishing. Impressive from the beginning, she was double chawed in colliering and weather, just as I was as a young owl. Fritha has proven herself time and time again, not just to me, but to all her rybs at the great tree. She has even received the highest merit badge a colliering chaw owl could earn.

When Fritha took her oath as a Guardian, I thought it would be the start of a life of discovery and adventure for a promising young owl. Little did I know that Fritha had already led a life of adventure, intrigue, and secrecy. I learned the truth from Fritha herself just recently, and I shall share it with you, my readers. She *feared the truth would make me mistrust her. On the contrary, it made me respect her even more.*

Fritha landed on an ice ledge in the tundra. To her relief, she had finally managed to cross the H'rathghar glacier. She was grateful to have gotten through the contrary winds known as the katabats as she had learned to do in the weather chaw. The flight was long and arduous. Being a Pygmy Owl, and an especially tiny one at that, she had to stop and rest many times. Even resting was no easy task in these parts — whenever she rested, she felt the deep northern chill down to her hollow bones, even though she fluffed out her down feathers to maximum fluffitude as her da had taught her to do. At least flying kept her warm, even if it tired her terribly quickly.

It was the dead of winter in the Northern Kingdoms, and a terrible time to be traveling there. But it was the only time she was able to get away. The owls of the Great Ga'Hoole Tree had just celebrated Long Night, and a short period of relative quiet would ensue. She hated having to leave the tree, but she would have hated to miss this trip even more. Fritha had told everyone that she was visiting her aunt on Elsemere Island at the

Glauxian Sisters retreat. It wasn't entirely a lie, she did stop there to visit with Aunt Bea for a night. But she didn't tell anyone the whole truth, either.

She took to the air again. Any owl watching her would have figured out that she was searching for something. It was daytime, and she circled low over the land. Fritha knew there were no crows in this region, and flew without fear of being mobbed. Her time was short, and she hoped that her search wouldn't take much longer.

Fritha turned her head slowly and surveyed the frozen landscape from the air. *There!* She finally spotted what she had been looking for. In the distance there was a pop of color — swirls of emerald and chartreuse — against the dull, colorless ground of the tundra. The colors could not be mistaken for the muted green of the shrubs and conifers found nearby; they were far too vivid. What Fritha was looking for, and found, was a dye basin — one that belonged to the kraals of the Northern Kingdoms.

It would not be wise to continue on as a plain-feathered owl, Fritha knew. The kraals, or pirates, of the Northern Kingdoms customarily dyed their feathers in garish hues. Purples, reds, yellows, greens, blues — the brighter the better. To be a natural shade of tawny brown, black, white, or gray would, ironically, make an owl conspicuous here. And you did not want to be conspicuous among the kraals. Kraals were the thugs of the Northern Kingdoms, and their bad reputation was well deserved. They fought for no side. They fought to steal, often to capture for ransom, and sometimes — Fritha hated even to think of it — to kill. They were more dangerous than hireclaws, who worked alone and fought for any side willing to pay them, because these pirates stuck together as a band, and thus had become much more advanced in their attack strategies.

Fritha landed next to the dye basin. She pulled a feather from her starboard wing. *What a shame,* she thought, *that one would have made a fine quill.* She dipped it carefully in the green dye and began painting the top of her head. *Always take extra care when painting your head and face; don't just go dipping your head into the dye unless you want to look like an ugly parrot.* She remembered those instructions well. When her head was painted in streaks of emerald and chartreuse, she worked on the rest of her body. She dipped both her wings in the dye and painted her chest. Then she painted the wings themselves. She hopped to a slab of issen vingtygg, or deep ice, that had been polished to a mirror finish near the dye basin. It was no surprise that such a mirror would be found here.

The kraals were infamous for their vanity, and kraals who just finished dying their feathers would want to take a good long look at the result. Fritha noted that the two shades of green were eye-poppingly bright — lurid, garish, and downright ostentatious. In other words, perfect. She knew that these particular shades were created using something called tundra nuggets mixed with the sap of pine trees and the oil from pine nuts. Other colors like reds and purples were made with various berries and flowers. If only the kraals put their dye-making knowledge to better use. She used similar dye- and paint-making techniques at the great tree, but she never used those dyes on her feathers; they were only used for illustrations in books. She took another long look at herself. Yes, she looked sufficiently kraal-like, she decided.

Fritha headed east, deeper into kraal territory. As she neared her destination, she spotted another dye basin off her port wing. This one was pink and violet. She made a quick circle over it. As much as she admonished the kraals' vanity, she did always like that shade of pink. There was no time to stop today to add another color to her already painted feathers. Fritha flew on. She knew she was but a few wing beats from her destination.

Though they were well hidden from view, the ground nests in which owls in this region lived were easy to spot for an owl who knew where to look. Fritha found the bulges of the nests in between and underneath the boulders that sat on the vast spongy surface. The mosses, lichens, and low shrublike plants that lived in the tundra made these nests quite comfortable.

Now, where was that nest? The boulders were hard to tell apart. As Fritha scanned the rock formations below, she saw an owl poke its head out from between two boulders. She guessed that it was a Long-eared Owl, but it was so elaborately painted in at least five different colors that it could have just as easily been a Striped Owl for all she knew. The Long-eared Owl eyed Fritha suspiciously, but then pulled back into its nest. Was that a hint of recognition Fritha saw in its eyes? *No matter,* Fritha thought, *you're not the kraal I'm looking for.*

Then, right beside an especially round boulder, another kraal emerged from his nest. There were very few Pygmy Owl kraals, and he was one of them. And he was the very pirate that Fritha sought.

Fritha landed on the round boulder, right in front of the kraal. She looked at him with wide eyes. He had dyed most of his feathers a royal blue, but at the very tips of his wings, there was a hint of pink.

"Well, look who has come to the Pirates' Lair," the Pygmy Owl said. The kraal extended his wings out to the side as if in flight. To Fritha's utter delight, the entire undersides of his wings were dyed her favorite shade of pink.

"Oh, Da, I'm so glad to see you!" Fritha exclaimed in her first language — a dialect of Krakish. She hopped toward her father and laid her head on his chest. "And you remembered my favorite color!"

"Of course, my love," Flinn greeted his daughter with joy in his voice. "I'm happy to see you, too! You are looking very fetching in green."

"I wouldn't think of arriving plain-feathered," Fritha said. "How did you know I was coming?"

"Oh, call it a father's gizzuition," he answered. "Now, come in. You must be famished. I've got a nice fresh lemming for you."

"A lemming would be splendid," Fritha replied happily. She was quite hungry, but had not realized it in her excitement to see her da. "I have so much to tell you, Da! I've been having the best time at the great tree. You wouldn't believe all the things I've learned to do!" The long trip was already worthwhile.

The two Pygmy Owls, father and daughter, disappeared into the ground nest, chatting excitedly.

Fritha was happy to be with her da. She would have liked to visit with her da for a full moon cycle, but she dared not be away from the tree so long. She would be missing too many chaw practices — the idea of missing even one chaw practice pained her; she couldn't imagine missing more. It had been almost a year since Fritha last visited her da in the Pirates' Lair. She would fit as much into her short visit as she possibly could, and the two talked into the dawn almost every night.

Still, she couldn't help missing the great tree. The season of White Rain would be in full swing, and she was looking forward to all the activity that came with it. She couldn't wait to get back to her nest and see all her friends. How different she'd felt about her first trip to the Great Ga'Hoole Tree, she thought. She was so young at the time that she barely remembered it. What she did remember was feeling immensely sad. She was being sent away from home, after all. She feared that she would never see her da again. And even though her da told her it was for her own good, she didn't fully understand why he was sending her away. And here she was now, being homesick for the tree.

Although she still didn't know why he had done it, how right her da had been to send her there! She was thriving at the tree — she was one of the best owls in the weather and colliering chaws, earning the highest merit badge a colliering chaw owl could earn, and she just loved writing for *The Evening Hoot.*

As much as she loved her da, her visits with him always reminded her that the kraal way of life was just not for her — the vanity, the disorderliness, not to mention the thuggishness. And when it came down to it, most of the kraals were just not that smart, and they didn't feel the need to get smarter, either. Her da was different in that respect. He was always inventing this and that, working out his "hypotheses." Even now, as Fritha watched him, Flinn was tinkering with a new formula for a dye that changed colors depending on the angle of the sun. He was much more like the owls of the Great Ga'Hoole Tree than he was his fellow kraals. The kraals realized this, too, and regularly left Flinn out of important activities. No one at the tree knew that Fritha was the daughter of a kraal, or that she would have become a kraal herself if it weren't for her da sending her away. It wasn't exactly that she was ashamed of where she came from . . . well, maybe she was, just a little bit.

As a newly arrived young owl at the tree, Fritha didn't dare talk about her kraal heritage. The Guardians' infrequent encounters with the kraals had never been amicable. The kraals' reputation, she learned, was worse than she had imagined. She had meant to tell her fellow Guardians the truth about her identity someday; she wanted to let them know where she came from and who she was. But night after night, season after season, she never found the opportunity or the courage. And now, she found herself leading this double life — sneaking away from the tree once or twice a year to see her father, inevitably telling lies in the process. With each visit, the lies and half-truths weighed more and more heavily on her gizzard.

As Fritha watched her da fiddle with his pigments, she wondered again why he had chosen to send her away to a life so different from his own.

"Da," she began gently, "why did you send me to the tree? Why didn't you keep me here and raise me as a kraal?"

Flinn didn't seem surprised by Fritha's question. He put down his mortar and pestle, and paused before he began his long answer.

"I was just a young owl myself when I first learned of the Great Ga'Hoole Tree," he said. "I had heard of it in songs sung by passing gadfeathers, but didn't know it was a real place with real owls until a raiding party returned one night with a certain little owl as a captive." He seemed lost in his memories as he spoke.

Flinn remembered clearly, he had been painting his feathers at a dye basin — red and turquoise. As he admired his own artistic creation, he spotted in his ice mirror a group of owls flying toward the lair. *Ah! Finally! They're doing it right!* The four kraals were flying in the formation he invented, correctly this time. He called it the VAT, short for Vacuum-assisted Transport. It was one of his proudest inventions. He got the idea when he was flying with a group of Snowies through some rough winds the previous winter. Being a Pygmy Owl in these parts had its challenges, and the katabats were one of the biggest ones. He realized, as he flew with the four much larger owls, that if they all positioned themselves a certain way, they created a small still space in their midst where the heaviest winds were blocked. He was able to get through the katabats that way. With further experimentation, he found that he could expand upon the idea. If the owls flying around the periphery flapped their wings in a certain rhythm, they created a vacuum in the space between them. Whatever was in the middle got sucked along. Flinn was very excited to tell the other kraals of his discovery. He had thought it would be a great way to transport injured owls or fledglings and smaller owls who couldn't fly through heavy gusts. But the kraals saw it only as a way to transport captives. *Typical.*

Flinn wondered who was being brought to the rock cell in the VAT. He saw that the owl in the middle of the formation was very small, even smaller than he was. It must have been an Elf Owl, he decided. An owl that size was in for a bad time in the Pirates' Lair. Until now, Flinn had been one of the smallest owls in the area. This prisoner's diminutive size intrigued him.

From the main room of the Pirates' Lair, Flinn could see into the stone cell where the Elf Owl was being kept. He chatted with the guards and they gave up all the information like gadfeathers at a grog tree. The prisoner was called Gylfie, and she came from the Southern Kingdoms. The kraals were holding her on behalf of some old Screech Owl who would be coming to question her.

The most fascinating thing Flinn learned was that the owl came from the Great Ga'Hoole Tree, and was in fact a Guardian of Ga'Hoole. He had heard stories about the Guardians — that they were a group of knightly owls that fought for justice and sought wisdom — but he never thought he would meet one, let alone have one brought to the Pirates' Lair with *his* invention.

For the next two nights, Flinn couldn't help but think about the little Elf Owl being kept in the rock cell. He wanted to know more about this Gylfie, but he had no business in the whole matter. He wasn't involved in guarding the prisoner — he was too small. Vlink and Phlinx, two dim-witted Snowies, were selected for that task. He wasn't involved in questioning the prisoner, either — he was not important or high-ranking enough. One of the Snowy captains was working with that creepy Whiskered Screech, Ifghar, on that task. What were they asking her? he wondered. As much as he tried to keep busy, his thoughts always fell to Gylfie and the Guardians of Ga'Hoole.

What was it like, he wondered, to live at the Great Ga'Hoole Tree? *I bet she's not left out of raids or missions. And I bet they don't laugh off her ideas.*

The very next day, Flinn got to know Gylfie a little better. Most of the kraals were out on a raid. Vlink and Phlinx were left behind to guard Gylfie, and Flinn was left behind to . . . well, Flinn was just plain left behind. He milled about in the main room of the lair hoping to catch bits of the conversation between the prisoner and her guards, or better, speak with the Elf Owl himself. But all he heard was Vlink and Phlinx going on and on about being left out of the raids.

Suddenly, he heard both Vlink and Phlinx gasp in awe.

"Look! Look!" said one.

"It's coming this way. By my talons, it can't be!" added the other.

Flinn tried to see what had caused this reaction, but couldn't. He tried to position his head so that he could hear as much as possible. But all he could hear was a bit of mumbling in a language he didn't understand. *Glaux?* Vlink and Phlinx were saying that Glaux had come to the Pirates' Lair to anoint them? *What rubbish! Just what's going on?*

Flinn had to see for himself. He left the main room of the lair and snuck around to the front entrance of the rock cell. He got there just in time to see an owl, who had been painted ear slit to talon in gold, cutting the Elf Owl loose. Ah, he suddenly understood. Vlink and Phlinx must have thought this golden owl was Glaux. What imbeciles! This owl was clearly just a regular Short-eared Owl who had found some of the prized golden sedge berries that the kraals were always on the hunt for. Flinn didn't know where to find the berries or how to make a gold dye himself, but he was smart enough to know that another owl might be able to. It became clear that the Elf Owl and the Short-eared Owl had executed a most cunning plan to trick Vlink and Phlinx into letting them go. Gylfie, clearly out-sized, had no hope of fighting her way to freedom; she used her wits instead. *That must be one smart little owl,* thought Flinn.

Gylfie and the golden owl were about to get away. Flinn knew he should try to stop them. The thing was, he didn't want to. He wanted to see Gylfie get away. He wanted to see if she could really do it.

Flinn looked to the western sky and realized that it was not gong to happen. He saw the rest of the pirates returning from the raid. The whole raucous crew was approaching, and fast! He was almost disappointed. It looked like Gylfie and her companion wouldn't get away after all.

But wait! What were they doing? Gylfie and the golden owl were moving the two great ice mirrors, the ones that were set up so that the kraals could admire their own image as they returned home. With considerable effort, the two owls tilted the two big slabs of polished ice to catch the sun. *I should really do something to stop them,* Flinn thought again, but he did not move.

Flinn watched as chaos filled the western sky. Beams of reflected sunlight blinded the approaching kraals. They were flying into one another and falling out of the sky! Flinn turned toward the east just in time to see Gylfie and her companion fly off. They made their getaway after all. Funny, Flinn found himself rooting for the prisoner rather than for his fellow kraals.

What a smart little owl! Flinn thought again.

After relating to Fritha the tale of the escape of Gylfie and the false, golden-painted Glaux, Flinn told his grown daughter that, many moon cycles after that valiant escape, he was impressed by another little owl.

It was the night of a full moon. Flinn was watching the diminutive egg in his nest rattle, gently at first, then with increasing urgency. *It's almost time!* He could hardly believe it. This was the little egg that was never supposed to hatch. When Flinn's mate laid this egg, she immediately saw that it was flawed — it was very small, even for the egg of a Pygmy Owl, and had a long thin crack that ran from top to bottom. Damaged eggs don't hatch, she told Flinn.

For a while, he thought it was just as well. His mate, Freya, had insisted on going on a raid with the rest of the kraals, and she never made it back. He wasn't surprised; Freya was always taking risks. She was a kraal through and through — as fierce as an owl ten times her size. He admired that, but he feared it, too. He feared he would lose her one day. And he did. He missed her dearly.

Flinn did not push the tiny flawed egg out of the nest, as Freya had told him to do. He couldn't do it, at least not until he knew for sure that it wasn't a hatcher. So, he had taken care of it, kept it warm, and surrounded it with the softest down he could pull from his own chest. *You never know,* he figured, *the little egg might have a chance.*

And now, it was going to hatch!

Just as Flinn leaned in to take a closer look, the crack that had always been on the egg grew wider. Pop! A tiny spur sprang out of the egg, making a tiny hole in the shell. The shell split along its crack. Out fell the tiniest little chick Flinn had ever seen, wet and glistening, with a head as big as the rest of its body. He took one look at his daughter and decided that Fritha would be her name.

The egg that wasn't supposed to hatch did. Fritha opened her beak and made a noise so loud that it could have come from an owl ten times her size. She looked at her da with big, curious eyes that seemed to be thinking already. Flinn was in love.

On the day Fritha became fully fledged, Flinn took her to the nearest dye basin in the tundra at dawn and taught her how to paint her own feathers.

As they went over how to apply dye to one's own head, Fritha asked, "Da, why do we paint our feathers?"

"Because the colors look nice," he answered. "Don't you like all the colors, Fritha?"

"I like the colors," Fritha said hesitantly. "It's just that ... brown and gray are colors, too, aren't they? What's wrong with them?"

"Nothing, dear."

"Then why do we cover the brown and gray of our feathers with all these other colors?"

What an inquisitive little owl, thought Flinn, *always asking why this and why that.* She left no question unasked, and no answer unchallenged. She was his daughter through and through. He had to think about the answer carefully, because it was bound to lead to a lot more questions.

"It's how we make ourselves unique, and how we push the boundaries of our owlness," Flinn had finally said.

"The colors do that?"

"Yes." Flinn thought a little more and added, "It's what's called an art."

"An art." Fritha nodded, seeming to understand. She applied the pink and vermilion dyes over her head with care, just as her da was showing her to do.

A few days later, Flinn found Fritha playing with a small chunk of ice from a broken ice mirror. She held it this way and that in her talons, examining it. She tilted the smooth, triangular chunk of ice, catching the light of the setting sun. When she held the ice at a certain angle, the sunlight burst through it, splitting into a rainbow.

"Look, Da!" she exclaimed, holding the prism steady in the light so that Flinn could see what she saw.

"Lovely, my dear!" he replied.

"They're all here, Da!"

"What's there, Fritha?"

"Colors! Red, orange, yellow, green, blue, violet . . . All the colors you'd ever want to see," she answered. Then she added, "You don't need sedges and berries to make colors. You can have all the colors your want in this little chunk of ice!"

What a smart little owl, Flinn thought, and churred.

Fritha waved the ice in her talons excitedly. The sunlight reflected from the polished surface and hit Flinn right in the eye. For just a moment, he was blinded. He shielded his eyes from the beam with his wing. When he looked up again at his daughter, he was reminded of an owl from his youth — Gylfie, another smart little owl.

Flinn watched Fritha play with the chunk of ice until twilight, all the while thinking about what that Elf Owl might be doing at the Great Ga'Hoole Tree. They probably taught proper lessons there — lessons about how a chunk of ice could contain all the colors of the rainbow, lessons about the properties of mirrors and light. Here, a small owl like himself was often overlooked. But there, perhaps, they were valued and respected as much as the bigger owls.

Just then, a small raiding party flew toward them from the south. There was a huge commotion in the sky. The owls, a dozen or so of them, landed raucously, boasting of their spoils. Some of them looked to be painted a brownish red, but Flinn immediately knew that it was not paint or dye — it was blood.

Among them was a Screech Owl named Drusilla — one of Fritha's young friends. She was but half a moon older than Fritha, and was already going out on raids. Fritha had been quite taken with the slightly older owl. Drusilla was covered in dried blood, and proud of it.

"I wish you could have seen me, Fritha," Drusilla bragged. "I was ferocious!" She mimed slashing at another owl with her talon.

"I'll bet!" Fritha replied excitedly.

Flinn saw Fritha's eyes light up as she listened to Drusilla boast about having killed an owl for the first time. He wilfed. In that moment, Flinn knew that he would not, could not, let his daughter become like that.

The next night, Flinn brought Fritha to the hot springs south of Pirates' Lair. He found a small pool of tepid water in a natural depression in the ground.

"Tonight, I will teach you how to wash all that dye off your feathers," he told her.

"So that I can dye myself different colors next time?"

"No, Fritha." Flinn had been thinking about his daughter and the great tree all day, and he had brought her here for a reason. "I don't think you'll want to paint your feathers for a while."

Fritha looked at him with inquiring eyes.

"You know that in other parts of these kingdoms, owls don't paint their feathers at all," Flinn continued.

"No other owls in all of the Northern and Southern Kingdoms paint their feathers, only we kraals do." Fritha repeated one of the things that her father had taught her.

"That's right. And what if I told you that I think you would be happy in one of these other places?" Flinn didn't know exactly how to tell his daughter what he was planning, but he went on. "I knew of an owl once, a little owl like you and me, who was as smart as any owl I had ever met. She came from a place far away from here, a place called the Great Ga'Hoole Tree. It's in the Southern Kingdoms. . . ."

"What are you trying to say, Da? Am I going away?" Fritha asked nervously.

Of course Fritha figured out his meaning immediately. She began to wilf, making herself even tinier than she already was. The last thing Flinn wanted to do was to make his daughter sad, but he had made up his mind.

"Yes, Fritha. I'm sending you away to a better place." He girded his gizzard, and had answered emphatically.

"Sending? Does that mean you won't be coming with me?" She wilfed completely.

Her sadness broke his heart. "No, dear, I won't. I'm an old kraal. What would the Guardians want with the likes of me?" he said wistfully. "I've lived all my life at the Pirates' Lair, and, maybe, despite living on the fringes as I do, this is where I belong. But you . . . you deserve better." He knew she would find little comfort in his words now, but he was sure he was doing the right thing. He went on. "That little owl I knew from the Great Ga'Hoole Tree was named Gylfie. She was the smartest owl I had ever met until you came along. You're smart, Fritha, and this," he gestured to the tundra, "is not where you belong."

When Fritha was done washing the dye from her feathers, she and Flinn flew a little ways farther south and met an old gadfeather friend of Freya's. Flinn introduced the Snowy to his daughter as "Aunt Bea."

Before father and daughter parted ways, Flinn gave Fritha a little dose of courage.

"You're going to do great things at the great tree, Fritha," he added as she and Aunt Bea were about to take off. "Don't forget where you came from. And remember that you can always come home."

Flinn was quiet for several moments after telling his long tale to his grown daughter. She was not a little owlet anymore, and deserved to hear the story from him.

"So now you know. Do you forgive me for sending you away?" he asked, fixing his aged but still-bright eyes on her.

"Forgive? There is nothing to forgive, Da," she replied with the slightest tremor in her voice. "I thank you, from the bottom of my gizzard."

It was getting late. The sky was beginning to grow light above them. They both knew that it was almost time for Fritha to head back to the great tree — her home. She would need a good day's rest for the long and arduous journey ahead. They bid each other goodlight and nestled down close for one last sleep before her departure.

Fritha was on the final leg of her return journey; she needed only to cross the Sea of Hoolemere to reach home. She rested one more time. Funny how she thought of the tree as home now, despite having been hatched in the Pirates' Lair. While it felt good to be heading back, Fritha dreaded having to tell all her friends and rybs about her "visit with Aunt Bea." She wished she could just tell them about her da — about what a great owl he was, and how much fun she had visiting him. It occurred to Fritha then, too, that her da ought to be able to see how she lived as a Guardian at the great tree, that he ought to see for himself just how right he had been to send her away.

No more hiding! Fritha made up her mind as the Great Ga'Hoole Tree came into view over the horizon. She shouldn't be ashamed of who she was or where she came from. She shouldn't have to sneak off to spend time with her da. Sure, he was a kraal, but he was a kraal whom she loved and was proud to call Da. Fritha would tell everyone at the tree where she came from and who she was. The very thought lifted her, and her flight seemed instantaneously effortless. She glided toward the light of her hollow.

When Fritha returned to the tree, she told us all of the double life she had been leading. It initially came as a shock to many — our very own Fritha, a kraal! But it did not make anyone think less of her. I, for one, could not be more proud of her. She has reminded me that no matter where we come from, we can grow in knowledge, virtue, and wisdom.

So far is Fritha from hiding her past that, one night, I spotted her with a single primary feather dyed pink. She told me it was to mark the anniversary of her arrival at the great tree.

I am pleased to inform my fellow Guardians and reading creatures everywhere that I just placed the following announcement in The Evening Hoot:

FLINN, A KRAAL OF THE NORTHERN KINGDOMS,
TO GUEST LECTURE AT
THE GREAT GA'HOOLE TREE

THE SEARCH-AND-RESCUE CHAW HAS A YEARLY TRADITION OF HOSTING A SPECIAL GUEST LECTURE SERIES, GIVEN BY AN OWL ACCOMPLISHED IN THE FIELD OF

SEARCH-AND-RESCUE SCIENCES. THIS YEAR, THE GUEST LECTURER WILL BE FLINN, A PYGMY OWL AND KRAAL FROM THE NORTHERN KINGDOMS. FLINN SPECIALIZES IN VACUUM-ASSISTED TRANSPORT, OR VAT, A METHOD OF TRANSPORTING INJURED OR OTHERWISE FLIGHT-CHALLENGED OWLS THROUGH THE MANIPULATION OF AIR CURRENTS. FLINN IS THE FIRST KRAAL INVITED TO LECTURE AT THE GREAT TREE. IN ADDITION TO HIS LEC-TURE ON VAT, HE WILL TEACH SMALLER SEMINARS ON KRAAL HISTORY AND CULTURE, INCLUDING THE ARTS OF DYE MAKING AND FEATHER PAINTING. THIS EVENT IS OPEN TO OWLS OF ALL CHAWS AND IS AN EXCELLENT OPPORTUNITY FOR KNOWLEDGE SHARING. ALL OWLS ARE ENCOURAGED TO ATTEND. FURTHER, IT HAS BEEN DECIDED BY UNANIMOUS VOTE OF THE PARLIAMENT THAT AFTER FINISHING HIS SERIES OF LECTURES, FLINN IS INVITED TO TAKE UP RESIDENCE AT THE GREAT TREE IN THE HOLLOW ADJOINING THAT OF HIS DAUGHTER, FRITHA.

THREE

Uglamore Redeemed

As a Guardian, I have known my share of noble and great owls. Some followed the honorable way from their first ceremony to their last, but others took a meandering path, finding nobility and goodness only at the end.

I knew almost nothing of the brave owl named Uglamore until the time of his death. There I was, in the Beyond, witnessing one of the most heroic sacrifices ever known to owlkind. Until then, I had thought Uglamore was a just simple thug from the abominable Tytonic Union of Pure Ones. It was only with the help of Coryn, Gwyndor, Doc Finebeak, and several dire wolves who I shall not name that I was able to piece together his story. In the last moon cycle of his life in the Beyond, Uglamore, alone, tired, full of revulsion at the course his life had taken, spoke his despair into the bonfires of those other lonely creatures — the gnaw wolves of the Sacred Watch. They heard his mutterings and monologues, and later related them to me. On returning to the great tree, I spent hours in Coryn's hollow, listening to his recollection of "Uncle Uglamore." Coryn spoke of him with love and admiration.

I hope now that Uglamore's story is known, the rest of the world's free creatures will as well.

He was tired. His feathers were tattered. He no longer had the strength to preen himself, and had not the company of other owls to do it for him.

The old Barn Owl named Uglamore was perched on an outcropping just beyond the dancing flames of the gnaw wolves' bonfire. Thoughts, memories, regrets assailed him. He hardly knew when he was speaking aloud to the flames, and when his words sounded only in his mind. Some memories seared his gizzard with shame and he tried to veer from them. Others were merely annoying. A precious few were tender.

Just now he was thinking about the name he was given at his hatching, as he often did these days when finding himself alone. He had almost forgotten it in all his years of soldiering. Bartholomew. How he had hated that name. Even worse was what his mother used to call him when he was a chick: Bartimoo. He shuddered as he remembered the sound of her voice as she said that word, and shook out his primaries reflexively. His father had also been Bartholomew, so had his grandfather, and his great-grandfather before that. As a young owl, he had always been disappointed that his parents couldn't come up with something more creative, more original.

When he and his mum first joined the Tytonic Union, he was still a fledgling. His father had just died, and his mum had told him how nice it would be to join other "like-minded" owls. Bartholomew was one of many young Barn Owls who were new to the Pure Ones. He had told all his new friends that his name was Shadow. After all, he had come from the southern edge of the Shadow Forest, where his family lived in a hollow of a pine tree on the bank of a pond. In fact, he had gotten to like the sound of the name — dark, mysterious, and formidable, perfect for a young ruffian such as himself, and perfect, too, for a newly pledged Pure One.

But Bartholomew would soon find out for himself that it didn't matter what name he came up with, he would be given a new one by the Tytonic Union. And that new name would define him as a full-fledged member of the Pure Ones. *Whatever it is, it* has *to be better than Bartimoo*, he had thought at the time.

He thought long and hard about the perfect Tyto Alba name. It certainly wasn't Bartholomew. Shadow was good, but not great. He wondered what the High Tyto's real name was — owls only called him High Tyto or His Pureness. Whatever it was, Bartholomew decided, it must have been fierce-sounding and very pure. The perfect name for a Tyto Alba, Bartholomew decided, was *Tytus* — the ultimate name for a Barn Owl and a devoted Pure One such as himself. He considered Albus, too, but decided that it sounded too meek.

As the occasion of his naming neared, he tried to drop hints, and he probably wasn't too subtle about it. Once, when he knew the High Tyto to be within ear-shot, he said rather loudly to one of his fellow young recruits, "You know what I think is a fantastic name for a soldier of the Tytonic Union? Tytus. Wouldn't it be a great honor to the High Tyto to have a loyal servant named Tytus?"

His companion, another Barn Owl called Junior, looked at him like he was a warbling idiot. And His Pureness, the High Tyto, flew off without paying Bartholomew even a modicum of attention.

The night of his naming finally came after Bartholomew and his mum had been with the Pure Ones for many seemingly endless moon cycles. He was as excited as a chick at his First-Meat-on-Bones cere-mony and slept barely a wink the day before. He remembered some of his Firsts in the old days in the Shadow Forest, and how special those ceremonies made him feel. But to the Pure Ones, the naming warranted no ceremony, it was just another task to be carried out. As the moon rose in the sky, High Tyto and his mate appeared before the three owls who were to be named — Bartholomew, Junior, and one other young Barn Owl.

"It is time for the three of you to begin your proper training as full-fledged Pure Ones," the High Tyto began. "From now on, you will only be known by your Tytonic Union names and will forget any previous name you have ever had." His mate gave a disinterested nod.

The High Tyto approached the owl known as Junior. "You will henceforth be known as Stryker."

Junior nodded and bowed his head. "I will not let you down, High Tyto."

Stryker — a good name, a powerful name, thought Bartholomew.

"You," the High Tyto was now addressing the Barn Owl next to Bartholomew, "you will henceforth be known as Wortmore."

Wortmore?! What kind of name is Wortmore? Bartholomew almost let out a churr. Oh, it would have been a bad time to be caught churring, and he knew it. Wortmore bowed his head, just as Stryker had.

At last, the High Tyto landed in front of Bartholomew. The young owl felt as if his gizzard was about to climb out of his body through his beak. *This is it*, he thought,

I'll finally be free of this horrid name. Good-bye Bartholomew! Good-bye Bartimoo! Come on, Tytus, say Tytus....

"And you," the High Tyto leaned in. Bartholomew's eyes widened with anticipation. "From this night forward, your name shall be Uglamore."

Bartholomew's only response was to yarp a pellet right in front of the High Tyto. It almost hit His Pureness in the chest. The young Barn Owl was stunned. "Sorry, High Tyto ... I mean, thank you. Thank you, High Tyto, I'm ... I'm honored, Your Pureness."

If there was a name worse than Wortmore, worse than Bartholomew or even Bartimoo, the High Tyto had found it.

Uglamore I was named, and Uglamore I became.

Over the years, Uglamore had gotten used to being called by his Tytonic Union name. He even liked it some days, like when Nyroc said it. In fact, many things seemed to change after the little chick was born. When he was merely days old, he had tried to say "Uglamore," except, in the garbled speech of the tiny owlet, it sounded more like "Oolamoo." It brought warmth to Uglamore's old gizzard.

How carefully had the name Nyroc been chosen for him, Uglamore recalled. When Nyra had first laid the egg, the "Sacred Orb" as she had called it, she had desperately wanted the hatch day to fall on the night of an eclipse. Because then, the little chick would join a most exclusive group: the Nyrolian owls, those owls hatched during an eclipse.

As the night of the eclipse neared, Nyra became fixated on the egg.

Uglamore was sure that Nyra had pecked at that egg to cause it to hatch before it was truly ready — an act that only the worst of owl mothers would even consider. It was the first of many perversions she would practice, Uglamore thought grimly: hate instead of love; mindless obedience instead of free thought; murder instead of friendship. He had felt sorry for the little chick even back then.

Just before the sun climbed over the horizon, Nyra announced that her son had hatched. Nyroc, she predictably called him, after herself. Maybe Uglamore shared a bond with Nyroc because they were both destined to their names — he after his father and his father's father, the young chick after his mother. Or perhaps he felt the bond because he and Nyroc were both fatherless. Who can say for sure? What he was certain of was that he felt an attachment to this chick that he could not explain, an attachment that was stronger than any he had felt since he joined the Tytonic Union of Pure Ones. What was more peculiar was his sense that this chick was different from any others he had ever known. When Nyroc looked into Uglamore's eyes, Uglamore felt as if his gizzard were being scoured, but it was a gentle scouring, so unlike the caustic gaze of the little one's mother, Nyra. He felt like his truest self — whatever that was — whenever he was near the hatchling. These were strange thoughts for a Pure One, that he knew.

Maybe because that connection was clear to all those who saw them, or maybe just because his best fighting days were behind him, Nyra began to entrust little Nyroc to Uglamore's care. Nyroc needed a father figure, anyone could see that, and Uglamore was happy to take on that role. She even told the chick to call him "Uncle Uglamore" — a title he outwardly objected to among the lieutenants, but inwardly held dear. Stryker had mocked him, calling him "Colonel Broody." He shook that off like rain on his feathers.

Since the original Tytonic Union of Pure Ones was reduced to remnants through their defeat in the battle known as The Burning, his job as "Uncle Uglamore" became more important to him than even achieving the rank of colonel — a goal that he had had since before he got the name Uglamore. Thankfully, when Nyra wasn't hags-bent on training Nyroc to be the perfect Pure One, she entrusted him to Uglamore without question.

As the hatchling grew, it became abundantly clear that Uglamore was more like a father to him than his real father, Kludd, could ever have been. Uglamore's own father had died before little Bartholomew's First-Meat-on-Bones ceremony, and Uglamore scarcely remembered the owl these days. His mother had kept him fed and safe, but she didn't do much beyond that.

Nyra was a different breed of mother entirely. She saw her son as a weapon that needed to be forged and honed rather than as a little owl who needed love and caring.

On the occasion of Nyroc's first flying lesson, Nyra berated him for being too slow and too loud. *Unbelievable,* thought Uglamore, the chick had flown better on his first try than most owlets do after half a moon cycle of lessons. He couldn't help but feel sorry for the little one, and he couldn't help but grow weary of Nyra and her ways. Her expectations for Nyroc and the way she treated him made Ulgamore's gizzard shudder. He remembered clearly the little one's sadness.

"I'll never be as good as Mum. . . . I mean, as General Mam wants me to be. And all these owls my own age think I'm a Goody Two-claws," Nyroc had complained to Uglamore before lighting down in his nest.

"Don't mind them, Nyroc. There are owls other than these, owls who know better."

Nyroc looked at him questioningly. "What do you mean, Uncle Ulgamore?"

What did *I mean?* Uglamore realized right then that he had been thinking about the Guardians of Ga'Hoole when he was speaking. Sure, there were owls other than the Pure Ones, but had he gone yoicks to be telling the little one that *those* owls — of whom it was forbidden even to speak — were better? *Those* owls, who had outsmarted and practically obliterated the Pure Ones during the Battle of the Burning? *Those* owls, who did not have the rigid social structure that the Pure Ones had? But maybe, if Nyroc were being raised by *those* owls, he'd be all the better for it.

Uglamore brought himself up short: That kind of thinking was bound to get him into trouble. *No,* he thought at the time, *I can't let myself think that way*.

"Nothing, Nyroc. I just meant that I know you'll do better next time."

That was the beginning of the end of Uglamore's devotion to the Pure Ones. He didn't realize it at the time, but now, as he bided his time in the Beyond, it was as clear to him as the night sky. His final betrayal of the Tytonic Union would come not much later.

It was after Nyroc's failed Special — the Tupsi, they called it, which was short for Tytonic Union Pure Special Initiation. That poor young Sooty, Dustytuft, was dead — murdered by Nyra. Uglamore had wanted to save Dustytuft, and to spare Nyroc the awful ritual, but he hadn't the courage to oppose Nyra openly. And he'd said nothing when Nyra set the famed tracker, Doc Finebeak, on Nyroc's trail.

Uglamore had terrible memories of his own Tupsi. He had been instructed to kill his cousin — his da's brother's son — also named Bartholomew, who had been a mere hatchling at the time. Uglamore was brought back to the Shadow Forest to do the deed. His mum had told him that he must prove himself to become a soldier of the Tytonic Union. She said that not only would he be committing an act of personal sacrifice, he would also be "putting that poor thing out of his misery." In her mind, the owlet would have led an "impure" life, so why should he have lived at all? With her urging, Uglamore shoved the still flightless owlet from his nest high atop a fir tree. He felt utterly confused and miserable afterward. He was being praised by his mum and his fellow Pure Ones for completing his Special. They told him how proud he should have felt. But the thought of his poor little cousin falling to his death had made him sick to his gizzard. He didn't sleep for a moon cycle.

Unlike Uglamore, Nyroc had refused to murder his friend. He fled from the canyonlands as a result. He flew north on tattered wings. When Uglamore learned of this the next night, he was so afraid that the young owl might fall out of the sky on those sad, de-feathered wings, that he took off in pursuit without a command from Nyra. It was an act of defiance, for sure. But Nyra, in her ever-self-important frame of mind, had interpreted it as an act of courage. She actually believed that Uglamore had gone after Nyroc in order to bring him back to her. "Yes, good, Uglamore! Get that little ingrate! I'll make you colonel yet!" she called after him.

Uglamore was not the best tracker, but Nyroc's trail was not hard to find. The poor owl was still losing feathers. Worse, he was losing blood. *Blood!* When Nyroc had refused to harm Dustytuft, Nyra flew into a rage and savagely slashed her own son's face. The sight of his blood made Uglamore's gizzard lurch. He tracked through the night, northward. He almost didn't notice that he had arrived in a forest. The sun had risen, but tall pine and spruce trees cast long, dark shadows. From the floor of the deep forest, Uglamore could barely tell that it was morning.

It had been a lifetime since he had been there, but there was no mistake, this was where he came from. *Ah, the Shadow Forest!* Uglamore was home.

Uglamore followed Nyroc's trail as far as the pond, then the trail disappeared. Snow had begun to fall and covered up any clues Nyroc might have left as to his whereabouts. Uglamore looked into the pond, the edges of which had started to freeze. He remembered looking at his own reflection in that very pond as a hatchling. How he had admired his own heart-shaped face and black eyes. "Tyto alba through and through," his mum had said of him. Uglamore glanced into the water again. He could hardly recognize himself. The years he spent with the Pure Ones had not been kind to him. His face had grown thin. The once-smooth outline of his face, where the white feathers of his facial disc met the brownish ones, had become broken and ragged. He couldn't help but think he looked like a mean old owl, the kind of owl that hatchlings stayed away from but made fun of when they were out of earshot.

He looked up at the trees around the pond. Would he recognize the one that he once called home? No, he decided. None of the trees looked remotely familiar. He had only vague memories of this place, and besides, the landscape must have changed since his hatchling days. In fact, just on the other side of the pond, a tree had toppled in a recent storm. He wondered if that could have been where his hollow was. He flew toward the fallen tree out of curiosity. The tree had many hollows and smaller holes. *I suppose this could have been my home,* Uglamore thought. He approached a hollow about halfway up the trunk, and poked his head in. Uglamore jumped back instinctively. *An owl!* Owls did not go poking into the hollows of strange owls. He didn't think any owls would occupy the hollow in an uprooted tree. *But those feathers . . .* He knew those feathers. *Nyroc!*

The poor hatchling must have been exhausted from his journey. Who wouldn't be, having flown all this way on tattered wings? Nyroc did not stir as Uglamore poked his head into the hollow once more. He had found him after all. He had followed Nyroc to make sure he was okay. Now that he saw that he was, Uglamore didn't know what to do next. Would he join Nyroc on the run from Nyra? He decided he couldn't. He might be of help to Nyroc now, but once the young owl grew stronger, Uglamore would only slow him down by staying with him. Should he just turn around and go back to the Pure Ones? Was that the only way for this old owl? No, he could not. There seemed to be no place in this world for the old warrior.

Nyroc slept peacefully on a bed of moss, his chest rising and falling with each breath. As Uglamore watched the young one, the light reflecting off of the fallen snow played a trick on his old eyes. From where he was standing, it looked as if there was a crown of light atop the sleeping hatchling's head. He had heard of just such a crown in the forbidden legends of Ga'Hoole — the crown that marked the true king! The sight sent a shiver through Uglamore's feathers. He blinked twice to clear his eyes. When he looked again, the crown of light was still there, and it was even brighter. He extended his wing as if to touch it, but pulled back. His gizzard told him there was something magical about this sight.

Uglamore was so lost in his thoughts that he had not heard the disturbance in the air. *What's this? Company.* Two owls approached the fallen tree on which Uglamore perched: first, a Masked Owl, and then, a Barn Owl who was all too familiar. Stryker, the best tracker the Pure Ones had, and one of his minions. Uglamore looked over at the hollow where Nyroc was sleeping. It was but a few wingspans away. *They'll see him for sure,* Uglamore thought. It appeared that he had led the Pure Ones right to the young'un. *Too late to fly away,* he lamented.

Stryker and his companion, the Masked Owl named Vaygar, landed on the root of the fallen tree.

"No luck finding him, eh, Uglamore?" Vaygar said.

"What did I tell you, Vaygar?" Stryker scoffed. "Colonel Broody couldn't find a brown mouse on a field of freshly fallen snow."

Ah, they haven't seen him! Maybe there's still a chance for Nyroc. "No sign of him, Stryker. But shouldn't you know that? Aren't you the tracker extraordinaire?" Uglamore hoped that the snow that was rapidly falling had covered up Nyroc's tracks — the ones he had followed just hours before.

Stryker ignored the flattery but seemed to puff up a bit. "I was on his trail until just south of here. Then this Glaux-forsaken snow began to fall. I saw some fresh tracks, but it was only you," Stryker complained. "I bet the coward headed east to Ambala, maybe even The Beaks. I'm losing him as we speak. I grow sick of tracking down this little brat. I wish General Mam had just killed the little wretch and been done with it."

"You're not going to find him here, Stryker." Uglamore couldn't believe that Nyroc was right under Stryker's beak, and the stupid owl didn't know it.

"So what are you doing here then?" asked Stryker.

Uglamore couldn't think of a good answer quickly, but Stryker decided he could answer his own question.

"Oh, right, *Shadow* of the *Shadow* Forest," he said mockingly. "Ha! Missed your childhood home, did you?" Stryker looked around. "By Glaux, what kind of owl would live in a place like this? I'll tell you, a pathetic one, that's who."

"I stopped here to hunt, if you must know," Uglamore lied. "And if you find this place so pathetic and offensive, then why don't you leave? Try to pick up Nyroc's trail, wherever you think he might have gone."

"I will. I'll find the hatchling before you do, that's for sure," Stryker replied.

Uglamore couldn't believe his luck! He might have saved Nyroc after all.

Vaygar had been quietly watching the exchange between his two superiors, although he wasn't giving them his full attention. He realized how hungry he had gotten when he thought he saw something tasty scuttle by.

"Let's go, Vaygar," Stryker commanded.

"If you don't mind, sir, I'd like to find a quick snack before we go. I'm starving, sir."

Stryker looked at the younger Masked Owl with indifference. "Suit yourself, soldier. You weren't of much help anyway. I'm headed east; I trust you'll catch up to me before too long." He shook out his primaries in preparation for flight.

"Yes, Commander Stryker, I won't be but a few moments," Vaygar replied as Stryker took off.

Great, thought Uglamore, just when he thought he was getting rid of them. At least Stryker was gone. He could deal with this soldier.

Vaygar turned his attention to Uglamore. "I'm ravenous," he said. "It's such an honor to be sent on this mission with Commander Stryker. I had to leave on short notice — didn't even have time for tweener. But I'll track better on a full stomach. With any luck, I'll catch up with the commander, and together, we'll bring that little brat back to General Mam. It might be just what I need to be promoted to lieutenant."

Such a thing will never happen, thought Uglamore. Not only would he do everything in his power to make sure that the "little brat" was left alone, but he also knew that the Pure Ones would never promote a Masked Owl to the rank of lieutenant.

"I think you'll find the best hunting on the other side of the pond," Uglamore suggested as Vaygar began to poke around the root of the fallen tree.

"Oh, no time for a proper hunt, Lieutenant. You heard Commander Stryker. I'll just catch a quick little snack."

"I think I saw a chipmunk just over there." Uglamore gestured toward a tree higher up on the bank. He saw that Vaygar was poking his head into this hole and that, getting dangerously close to the hollow where Nyroc was still sleeping.

"Nah, these little bugs will do," Vaygar insisted as he plucked juicy little insects from the rotting wood.

Just then, there was the faintest rustle from the hollow halfway up the fallen tree.

"What have we here?" Vaygar asked.

Uglamore knew it was Nyroc. He must have shaken his feathers as he slept — something that owls, and indeed many birds do, as they drift from deep to shallow sleep. He had to get rid of this nosy owl, fast.

"Had enough to eat, haven't you?" he asked. "I think you better try to catch up to Commander Stryker. You wouldn't want to keep him waiting."

"I wouldn't . . ."

But even as Vaygar said it, he peeked into the hollow where Nyroc was sleeping. And just as Uglamore had done, he jumped back.

"By Glaux! It's the hatchling!"

Still asleep, Nyroc had turned his head toward the opening of the hollow. There could be no mistake — the slash across his face made it clear that he was Nyra's son.

"Shh. Don't wake him," was all Uglamore said. He had a feeling in his gizzard that this was going to end badly. Just moments ago, he had been unsure whether or not to return to the Pure Ones in the canyonlands. Now, his choice was clear. He could not — would not — go back to his old life. And more important, he would not let the Pure Ones capture the young'un.

"You knew he was here all along, didn't you? I have to tell Commander Stryker!" Vaygar exclaimed.

Uglamore said nothing. He knew what he had to do. The old Barn Owl had nothing against the young soldier who was only trying to be loyal, only trying to please Stryker and Nyra in a futile attempt to climb the ranks within the Pure Ones. Uglamore's next act should have come easily to him; he had done it enough times in his service to the Tytonic Union. But this time, he felt more than a twinge of guilt, for this time, it was his will, not that of his commander. But what could he do — this was the only way he could save Nyroc. Vaygar never saw it coming. With one swift motion, Uglamore's talon ripped through his neck. The Masked Owl died instantly.

In that moment, Uglamore knew that his days as a member of the Tytonic Union of Pure Ones were over. His place was most definitely not at the side of Nyra as one of her colonels. But his place was not with the hatchling, either.

When Nyroc awoke the next evening, he saw no sign of any owl having been there. The world was white, having been covered in a thick blanket of snow. The snow concealed the blood that belonged to a soldier of the Pure Ones. It also concealed the tracks of his protector.

As he bided his time in Beyond the Beyond, Uglamore thought often of the last time he saw the hatchling in the hollow of that fallen tree. How helpless he had seemed, how vulnerable. It was only a few moon cycles ago, but it seemed like an eternity.

He never thought he would see Nyroc again, but there he was. He had spotted him that day at the carcass of the moose.

He avoided being seen by the young'un, but he heard much about his exploits by loitering at the edge of the gnaw wolves' circles. He learned that Nyroc had changed his name to Coryn. He learned that a Spotted Owl from the legendary Great Ga'Hoole Tree was tutoring him in the strange art of catching coals on the fly from the furious volcanoes of the Beyond. His weary heart rejoiced that the little owlet he had cared for in his last days as a Pure One had shaken free from that dark dominion.

One day, he saw him again. As Uglamore perched on an ice shelf in the Beyond, he watched the young Barn Owl once known as Nyroc circle the volcanoes. He could scarcely believe his old eyes. He was diving and rising with such ease, it astounded the old owl who once knew him so well.

The dire wolves whom he had befriended had been telling one another sensational tales of the special owl who would retrieve the ember. In the beginning, Uglamore gave little credence to their talk, thinking the dire wolves were overly dramatic and superstitious. But as he watched Coryn — always careful that the young one did not see him — he knew that it was all true. The young Barn Owl whom he had cared for as a father would a son was none other than the true heir to

King Hoole. And Coryn was about to prove himself by retrieving the Ember of Hoole.

Uglamore thought back to that night in the Shadow Forest where he saw Nyroc sleeping with a crown of light upon his head, and it all made sense.

Coryn. His name is Coryn now. And just like that, the young owl had done something that the old owl was never able to do — he had chosen his own name. *Remarkable. And you've chosen your own destiny, young'un. Perhaps I can still choose mine.*

Suddenly, howls and cheers from creatures of air and land filled Uglamore's ear slits. "The new king lives! Long live Coryn, Heir of Hoole!" Even a wandering caribou herd brayed, "Long live Coryn, the King!"

He had done it! Coryn had retrieved the legendary Ember of Hoole from the depth of the great volcano. It didn't matter that he was once the obedient son of a Pure One. It didn't matter that he never lived up to the name given to him at his hatching. He had rejected that name and all it meant. He had free will. The old Barn Owl wept with joy.

But what was this at the edge of Uglamore's tear-blurred vision? Nyra skulking in the shadows. The mother who had failed to turn her son to the vile ways of the Pure Ones was here to stop him from retrieving the ember — or worse! Uglamore scanned the creatures near and far for someone who might help. All were lost in rejoicing. Then, he caught the eye of the old tracker, Doc Finebeak. The tracker nodded and flew to Uglamore and lighted down at his side.

"She's going to do something," he said.

Uglamore nodded.

"She'll make a move soon. We have to be ready. Are you up to it?" the tracker asked the old lieutenant.

Uglamore was indeed ready. Ready to cast off his past with the Pure Ones along with the name they'd given him, ready to redeem the shreds of good still left in his own gizzard. Ready to give his life for a young king.

The rest of the story, I think you already know. Uglamore protected Coryn until the very end. When Nyra threatened to steal the Ember of Hoole from her son and kill him in so doing, Uglamore was there to stop her. He died valiantly in the process. He gave his life for the true king. And now that the full story of this brave owl is known, the legend of Uglamore can be told and retold by owls and wolves alike.

FOUR

Brothers Brave and Blustery

T avis and Cletus may not be familiar names to many in the world of Ga'Hoole, but for those of us who have gotten to know them, their colorful history and characters are unforgettable.

You know, of course, dear reader, the story of Twilight, one of the Band, who grew up an orphan after his mother, the renowned poet Skye, died mysteriously soon after his hatching. But did you know that Twilight has two older brothers? None of us, including Twilight, knew of the existence of these two Great Grays until recently. It was a jubilant reunion for the three brothers. And these same two brothers, Tavis and Cletus, were pivotal in our victory over the revitalized forces of Nyra and the Striga in the War of the Ember.

But there is much more to these two owls than their recent exploits. Since the War of the Ember, Tavis and Cletus have chosen to take up residence at the great tree, where they have been a font of knowledge — not necessarily academic knowledge, mind you, but practical knowledge that can be gained only from *living life in the open skies. We have shared many stories over tweener and tea; some have been sad, some funny, and many action-packed. Allow me to share one of these with you. On the surface, the brothers are brash and cocky. But I hope that after you read their tale you will realize that beneath the bluster they are virtuous and valiant.*

As the sun turned red and plunged toward the horizon in the Desert of Kuneer, Cletus awoke in his burrow and stretched his wings out to the side, one at a time. He did this every time he woke up; it had become a habit. It was still hot in the desert as the sun set, and by drooping and stretching his wings, Cletus exposed the unfeathered area under each wing, which cooled him slightly. It took him half a moon cycle's worth of sleepily bumping into the walls to learn that if he tried to stretch both wings, he could barely unbend his elbow joints.

Not many Great Gray Owls lived in ground burrows in the desert. In fact, Cletus knew of only two, including himself. The other was his older brother, Tavis. Ground burrows were usually occupied by much smaller owls. Cletus was painfully aware of this fact. He was particularly large for a Great Gray Owl. Tavis was even larger. It was a wonder that Cletus and Tavis found a burrow big enough to accommodate them. They guessed that it must have belonged to some foxes, or maybe a family of coyotes.

The two brothers were originally from the Forest Kingdom of Ambala. *Ah, Ambala.* They remembered the place fondly — so lush, so green, so different from this remote corner of the southwestern reaches of the Desert of Kuneer. This place was the very opposite of lush and green. The parched earth stretched as far as the eye could see. Trees were as rare as rain showers. The only plants were small shrubs and alien-looking cacti. During the day, the sun beat down on the pale earth and baked the surface of the landscape. At night, the biting cold set upon the land as quickly as an owl on a fat mouse. This was one of the areas of the desert where not many owls lived. Those who did live here mostly kept to themselves.

If Tavis and Cletus could have lived all their lives peacefully in the forests of Ambala, they certainly would have. Growing up, they had shared a comfy hollow in a large oak tree with their mum and da. One day, their da had gone out hunting and never came home. Their mum had found out that he was killed by one of the earliest leaders of the Pure Ones, known only as the High Tyto. Their father's death had been particularly devastating for the whole family because their mum had just laid an egg. Then, not a moon cycle later, their mum disappeared while Tavis and Cletus were out hunting. She had been sitting the egg in their nest. They had found her body a few nights later. Mum and Da had always been very outspoken against the notions of "owl purity" touted by the so-called Pure Ones; their mum and da said it loud and clear on many occasions: Owl purity was a load of racdrops. Tavis and Cletus had suspected that it was their opinions that got them both killed. The egg that their mum had been sitting looked as if it had hatched, but the brothers had found no sign of the chick.

After that, Tavis and Cletus knew that their days in Ambala were numbered. The hollow they had shared with their parents was a constant reminder of their loss. The owls of St. Aggie's were still patrolling the area, stealing eggs and owlets and recruiting thugs. The Pure Ones were moving in as well, savagely targeting any owl who disagreed with their "philosophy." The two brothers decided that they had to leave Ambala for good.

For much of that summer, the two owls roamed the Southern Kingdoms, spending time in abandoned nests here and there. None had felt like home. And as vagabond owls, they continued to have run-ins with the Pure Ones and St. Aggie's patrols. When autumn came, Tavis and Cletus decided they needed to settle down. They found themselves in a wide, shallow, crater-shaped region in the Desert of Kuneer. Locals called it the "Broken Egg" for the jagged, packed earth ridges that rimmed the edges like fragments of an eggshell. Large, abandoned ground burrows were plentiful. The Pure Ones and St. Aggie's owls never ventured here. The land was vast and the brothers lived far from their nearest neighbors. The owls around here weren't very sociable, but they looked out for one another because they were together in their solitude. For the first time since their father's death, they felt safe. And so they stayed and made the ground burrow their home. That was years ago.

One evening, Cletus poked his head out of the burrow he shared with his brother Tavis. To the west, the last remaining glow of the sun cut the earth ridges black against the sky. The northern edge of the Broken Egg sloped up behind him, dimming into gray as stars began to dot the sky. His eyes adjusted to the twilight, and he looked for the larger Great Gray, who had already gone out to hunt. Prey was often hard to find here, and the brothers knew they would have to get started early. It was springtime, and many of the Burrowing Owl families in the desert were sitting eggs and hatching chicks, so there was a quite a bit of competition for food. But with any luck, Tavis and Cletus would find a nice plump pocket gopher — a desert delicacy.

As Cletus flew toward their usual hunting grounds, he spotted Saul, one of his Burrowing Owl neighbors. He was standing guard near his hollow. Cletus knew that this must mean Saul's mate, Trixie, had laid a clutch of eggs. It was customary for male Burrowing Owls to stand guard during the day as the females sat their eggs. Soon, Saul would also be on the hunt for food to bring back to the burrow.

Saul and Trixie had been Tavis and Cletus's first friends in the desert. They were very kind to the two Great Grays when they first arrived in Kuneer. They taught them the ways of desert living — how to find water in succulent cacti, how to hunt without the cover of trees, and how to clean their feathers by rolling in the sand. Cletus was reminded that if it had not been for Saul and Trixie, he and Tavis might have never been able to make a home for themselves here. He and Saul exchanged nods in polite greeting as Cletus flew on.

In his usual hunting ground, not far from his burrow, Cletus's brother Tavis was perched atop a tall cactus, sitting and waiting. Had he been in a forest, he would have been hidden from view by branches and leaves. But out here in the desert, he relied on being very still to avoid being seen by prey. He spotted a small burrow not twenty pytes away. It was a new burrow, he was sure it hadn't been there yesterday. *There's gotta be a pocket gopher in there,* he thought hungrily. Tavis and Cletus knew that no owl in his right mind would dig a burrow so close to an occupied burrow. Everyone around here prized their privacy. It had to be a prey animal.

Just then, Tavis heard a soft rustle. He looked toward the entrance of the burrow and saw the slightest movement. A small brown head poked out of the burrow, just above the surface of the sand. *Gotcha now, tasty!* Tavis crouched down ever so slightly and lifted off from his perch. He flew low to the ground with silent, slow wing beats. He extended his talons, ready to make the kill. Great Grays prided themselves on killing their prey with a single, powerful strike of their talons. When they were hatchlings and just learning to hunt, Tavis and Cletus had always been taught never to cause suffering. So, it was with a single-minded intent to kill that Tavis dove for the burrow.

Tavis was suddenly derailed when he heard a loud screech.

"OOOWL!"

The brown head quickly retreated back into its burrow. Tavis retracted his talons. But he had been flying in so fast that it made him lose his balance in midair. He landed face-first in the sand with a muffled thud.

"Sorry, brother."

It was Cletus.

Tavis stood himself up, more than a little peeved.

"That was an owl there in that burrow," Cletus said as Tavis dusted himself off. "Couldn't let you kill an owl."

"I thought it was a pocket gopher," Tavis grumbled. "Since when does an owl dig a burrow this close to ours? That just ain't right."

"Shh, here he comes."

The occupant of the burrow in question poked his head out again. Indeed, it was not a gopher of any kind, it was a Burrowing Owl. And this Burrowing Owl looked none too pleased to see Tavis and Cletus.

Cletus, always the neighborly owl, decided he would make the introductions.

"Hi there," he began. "Sorry about that. My brother here thought you were a pocket gopher."

"Yeah, sorry," Tavis added. "Not that you look anything like a pocket gopher now that I'm getting a good look at ya. It was hard to see, what with the setting sun and all. We didn't know you had dug this burrow."

The Burrowing Owl stared at the two Great Grays angrily and said nothing.

"I'm Cletus, and this is my brother Tavis," Cletus continued. "We live in a burrow just over there." He gestured toward their burrow.

There was another long, awkward pause.

"I didn't scare you, did I?" Tavis asked, tilting his head sheepishly.

The Burrowing Owl shot Tavis a look that told him he wasn't the type to scare easily. Finally, he opened his beak. "Well, Cletus, Tavis, I trust you'll know next time that I'm not some sort of prey animal." And without ever introducing himself, he withdrew back into his burrow.

The Great Grays had met their fair share of thugs, hooligans, and all-around bad owls in their lifetimes. But there was something about this owl that made both of them bristle.

"Seems we got ourselves a new neighbor," Tavis said to Cletus.

"Guess so, brother. I guess so."

A few nights later, Cletus and Tavis got a visitor. It was an old Burrowing Owl named Hiram who lived beyond the sand dunes a ways south. Hiram was a kind old soul who enjoyed his peace and quiet. The old owl seemed very concerned.

"Just wanted to check in with my fellow desert dwellers," Hiram started after the three owls exchanged some pleasantries. "Notice anything . . . unusual around your part of the desert?"

"Unusual how?" asked Tavis. While he didn't say it right away, he immediately thought of his and Cletus's encounter with their obnoxious new neighbor.

"Well, you know how I dug my hollow on a piece of unexcavated land? I came out here looking for a place where I can be on my own. That's what I had, until a few nights ago. Seems I got me some new neighbors."

Tavis and Cletus gave each other a meaningful look.

Hiram continued. "I found the opening of a new burrow not ten pytes from my own. So I went to investigate. There were two Burrowing Owls in there. They were real off-puttin', wouldn't tell me their names."

"Your story is starting to sound awfully familiar, Hiram," Tavis said.

"We have a new neighbor, too," Cletus piped up. "Burrowing Owl. Dug a burrow a pellet's yarp away from here."

"What else did you find out about the ones near you?" Tavis asked.

"Well, not much," Hiram answered. "As I said, they wouldn't tell me their names, hardly said a word to me, even though I was trying to be nice. Told me to mind my own business, else they might have to come over and mind it for me," he added indignantly.

The brothers felt bad for the old owl. He seemed truly troubled.

"Oh, I almost forgot," Hiram said, his voice growing in fervor. "It seems like they've been excavating night and day. I can hear 'em from my burrow. How much space could two Burrowing Owls possibly need? I swear to Glaux they're about to bust through my walls!"

"I thought I heard some excavating these last few days, too." Tavis turned to Cletus.

"There's definitely something odd about all this."

Tavis nodded with his brother in agreement. "I think we better figure out what's going on."

Hiram seemed relieved. "I thought I should tell someone."

"I'm glad you came to us, Hiram," Tavis assured him. "We'll get to the bottom of it. In the meantime, keep your eyes open, and let us know if you see anything else suspicious."

Later that very night, Tavis and Cletus went on a reconnaissance mission. The two owls flew side by side, slow and low over the land. Their eyes searched the surface, sweeping from left to right and then back again. They scanned the desert from the southwestern corner to the northeast. It took them the rest of the night and into the dawn.

The first thing they noticed was that there were a lot more burrows than there used to be. And most of the openings looked like they were freshly dug. When they looked closer, they realized that the burrows weren't randomly scattered across the desert as they might expect. On the contrary, they seemed quite regular, forming a sort of network. The brothers nodded to each other. They would have to talk about this once they got home.

As they neared their own burrow, they spotted something else strange. It was their new neighbor, the Burrowing Owl, dragging some food back to his hollow. But it wasn't just some food, it was a whole lot of food!

"How many mice do you think he's got there?" Cletus whispered to Tavis.

"Must be at least a dozen!" Tavis answered.

It was hard to tell because the Burrowing Owl had tied the tails of all the mice together into a knot, and was dragging the lot of them across the sand. It was an appalling sight. The bundle of prey was far larger than the owl. And he looked to be using all his strength to move the bundle.

"Well, that's just plain wrong," Cletus said.

"Disgusting," Tavis agreed.

It's an unwritten rule among owls that you never kill more than you can eat. Doing so was not only wasteful, but more important, it was disrespectful to the creature that gave its life. As far as the brothers were able to tell, this Burrowing Owl lived alone in his burrow. They never saw any signs of a mate or chicks. Even if there were chicks, twelve mice were more than enough to feed several families.

"This desert's never had too much in the way of prey; he may as well be taking those mice right out of some chick's beak," Travis said.

"Let's go have a little talk with our greedy neighbor," Tavis replied, angling down toward the owl.

The Burrowing Owl had spotted the two Great Grays a ways back. He was going as fast as his featherless legs would take him while hauling his heavy load. There was no place to hide around here. And now, there was no avoiding the interlopers.

"Pardon us, neighbor," Cletus began politely as he landed. "Remember us? Cletus, and my brother Tavis?"

The Burrowing Owl dropped his bundle of mice from his beak. "I remember. What do you two want?" he responded brusquely.

"That's an awful lot of mice you have there," Cletus continued in as polite a tone as he could manage.

"Yes, what of it?" the Burrowing Owl said, not hiding his annoyance.

"What army are you feeding?" Tavis tried to jape.

The Burrowing Owl's yellow eyes widened. He seemed alarmed, just for a second. Then, he regained his composure. "What does it matter? I've caught them. They're mine."

Tavis and Cletus looked at each other, not sure how to continue their line of questioning. Cletus finally asked, "You live alone in your hollow? That just seems like an awful lot of food for one owl. Prey is scarce around here, and . . ."

Before Cletus could finish, the Burrowing Owl interrupted. "What I do with the prey that I catch is my business. I suggest that if you're hungry, you go off and do some hunting of your own, instead of standing here and questioning me."

Tavis was getting angry, and without even realizing it, he began to puff himself up in a threat display. "We just figured we should know what's going on so close to our home," he said, gritting his beak. "We've been living in this desert for a long time, and when a stranger shows up and starts digging new burrows and hunting up all the prey, we have a right to know what's going on."

Tavis's and Cletus's sheer size should have intimidated any owl. But this Burrowing Owl, who was a fraction of the size of a Great Gray, was unmoved. With a steely glare in his yellow eyes, he told them, "All you need to know is that I'm an owl who does not take kindly to being interrogated." With that, he resumed hauling his heavy load.

Cletus and Tavis were once again at a loss. They just did not know what to make of this strange owl and his infuriating attitude.

Tavis realized that after two meetings, the owl still hadn't told them his name. He called out after the owl, "Hey, the least you can do is tell us your name!"

The Burrowing Owl decided that he would give them this much. Without turning around, he dropped his mice momentarily and said, "If you must know, the name is Tarn."

At the southwestern edge of the desert, Hiram was getting ready to turn in. He tucked himself into the back corner of his burrow and shut his eyes. As he began to drift off to sleep, he heard a loud and familiar scratching. His new neighbors were excavating — again!

"The nerve of some owls!" Hiram said to no one in particular.

He noticed that the source of the noise sounded closer than ever. He leaned his head toward the back wall of this hollow.

"It's all going as planned," Hiram heard an owl say.

"Excellent," replied another.

His beak dropped open in outrage. Hiram could hardly believe it — they had dug so close to his burrow that he could hear their voices right through the earth! He couldn't help but listen.

"Tarn will be pleased. As will Her Pureness. The army of the Pure Ones will be stronger than ever."

"The PURE ONES?!" Hiram couldn't help but say out loud.

The Pure Ones were infamous all over the Northern and Southern Kingdoms these days. Word had spread about their monstrous moonfaced leader and the terror she brought with her. Hiram had heard that they had recently been defeated, that what remained of them had been scattered throughout the Southern Kingdoms. Could it be that some of them were here in the Desert of Kuneer, just a thin earthen wall away?

As Hiram contemplated this, the owls on the other side of the wall fell silent.

Suddenly, dirt and sand exploded in Hiram's face. He fell back in shock. When he cleared his eyes, there was a Barn Owl crouched in front of him. Hiram had never seen a Barn Owl up close in all his days in the desert, much less in his own burrow. The Barn Owl lowered her head menacingly and squinted her brown eyes at the Burrowing Owl, who was half her size. Hiram instantly knew that the Barn Owl was not there for a pleasant chat. He turned to run. Before he could take a single step, the Barn Owl reached out with her talons and slashed at him. Hiram fell. Blood ran from his nape where she had cut him, and soaked into the earth. As he lay there, feeling the life drain from him, the Barn Owl smiled and whispered to him, "That's right, old-timer, the Pure Ones are here."

"I'm starving, brother. I'm beginning to wonder if I can eat a cactus," Tavis said to Cletus.

It was another night, and the two brothers were out on another hunt. It seemed as if they had been searching for prey for ages, flying low over the land in wider and wider circles. They had been used to the scarcity of food in their part of the desert, but this was becoming exhausting. There was not a mouse or a gopher to be found. They'd even settle for insects if they could find any of those. The last time they had seen their neighbor Saul, he told them he was afraid there wouldn't be enough food to feed his chicks when they hatched. It was a subject that worried all their fellow desert-dwelling owls.

All they had to do to figure out what happened to the prey was look down at the desert landscape. More new burrows had cropped up since their reconnaissance flight. There must be an influx of Burrowing Owls in this part of the desert. But it was baffling — owls usually went where the food was. Why on earth would all these owls move to this area when it had so little food to begin with?

Before they knew it, they found themselves at the southern edge of the desert. Tavis and Cletus landed on a cactus to rest. They had been flying for far too long on empty stomachs. The tumbleweeds were beginning to look like fat squirrels to them.

Out of the corner of Cletus's eye, he noticed movement from one of the burrows. He instantly turned his head to focus on whatever it was that moved. What he saw startled him — dark eyes on a white, heart-shaped face — the unmistakable face of a Tyto alba. This was most unusual — not only because Barn Owls were almost never found in the Desert of Kuneer, but also because Cletus recognized that particular burrow. The Barn Owl took off in silent flight toward the north, having not spotted the two Great Grays that perched nearby.

"Hey, Tavis," Cletus whispered to his brother, "ain't that Hiram's burrow over there?"

"I'm certain it is," answered Tavis.

"I must be seeing things on account of my being so hungry. I swear to Glaux I just saw a Barn Owl fly outta there."

"No, you ain't seeing things. I saw it, too."

As Cletus looked at his brother, Tavis wilfed ever so slightly. Cletus, too, felt an alarming twitch in his gizzard.

Silently, the two owls approached the burrow. They made themselves as small as they possibly could, which, by desert standards, was still huge, and crouched near the opening. They couldn't get a very good look into the burrow, but they heard an earful. It sounded as if there were dozens of owls in that burrow! They knew the burrow to be very small. But tonight, it sounded as if it stretched across the desert, underground.

Tavis and Cletus looked at each other. They knew that if they talked aloud, they'd surely be found out, so they kept quiet.

There was quite a commotion in the burrow. Several owls were trying to speak at once, and it was hard to make out what they were all saying. After a little while, however, the owls in the burrow began to settle down. One voice rose above the rest.

"What are we supposed to do about these desert dwellers?" an owl asked. "While they're here, we can't even go outside to stretch our wings without fear of being seen."

"Yeah!" another owl added. "This part of the desert is ours now, why are we still hiding?"

Hoots of agreement ensued.

"Quiet!" a voice called out.

Both Cletus and Tavis instinctively ruffled their feathers, lowered their heads, and assumed a defensive posture. They recognized that voice. *Tarn!* That nasty Burrowing Owl neighbor of theirs.

The owls in the burrow heeded Tarn's command and instantly became quiet.

"You are right," Tarn began. "This part of the desert *is* ours. We have worked tirelessly, excavating day and night. We have built up our forces without anyone knowing. From this hidden fortress we will launch a new assault on the kingdoms. We are on the brink of domination, once again!"

Cletus and Tavis wilfed. They knew they were on the verge of discovering something terrible.

Tarn continued. "It is time that we get rid of these desert-dwelling lowlifes for good! The Tytonic Union of Pure Ones has risen once again!"

Cheers erupted from all the owls in the burrow. Now, instead of dozens, it sounded like there were hundreds of owls.

"Should we begin driving out the remaining desert dwellers?" an owl asked.

"No!" Tarn answered definitively. "We cannot allow them to escape and tell other owls of our presence here. General Mam has ordered us to remain hidden. The rest of the owl world must not know that we have amassed our forces here. We still need time to prepare, per General Mam's instructions."

"Then, does that mean . . ."

Before the owl could finish asking his question, Tarn answered it. "Kill them, and take their burrows, just like

112

we did to that old fool who lived here. Exterminate them!" he bellowed.

The owls in the burrow hooted eagerly. Outside, Tavis and Cletus felt a hollow pull in their gizzards. *Hiram!*

"In two nights' time we will have finished connecting the southern and eastern networks of burrows." Then Tarn added, "With our tunnels linked we will be able to burst into all the remaining burrows at once. We'll slaughter these yokels and the desert will be ours. I want all squads in position the moment the tunnels are complete! We'll strike at dawn two days hence!"

Cletus had to keep Tavis from storming into the burrow then and there.

"Try to kill *me*? That bad-butt, skinny-legged, lousy owl wants to kill *me*? Well, I'd like to see him try! Why, I could just tear that owl wing from wing!" Tavis's anger was brimming. He couldn't believe what he had heard and seen. He and Cletus snuck their way to another burrow opening near Hiram's old home and looked in. They saw what must have been hundreds of owls — mostly Barn Owls, some Sooty Owls, Masked Owls, and a few Burrowing Owls — gathered in a freshly excavated chamber. Tunnel mouths pocked the edges leading to what had to be a vast network of burrows. The

Pure Ones — that loathsome lot was *here*, near *his* home, AGAIN!

Cletus tried to calm his brother down. He practically had to wrestle Tavis away from the burrow. He was just as furious as his brother, but he knew that rage would do them no good now. The brothers flew toward their burrow. Something had to be done.

"Think, Tavis, think! We can't just go attacking without a plan," he said. "We have more than ourselves to think about. They were talking about killing every owl who lives here! Think of the hatchlings, not to mention the eggs. Think of Saul and Trixie."

Cletus knew that, as big and powerful as they were, he and Tavis were only two owls against hundreds. Besides, where would that leave the rest of the desert dwellers? Most of them were Burrowing Owls who lived peaceful lives. Like Hiram, Glaux bless his scroom, many of them were old and weak. Others were mere hatchlings who had yet to take their first flight. They could never defend themselves against the forces of the Pure Ones. Cletus knew that he and Tavis would have to use their brains instead of talons in this situation. He was sure that, deep down, Tavis knew it, too.

When they reached their hollow, Tavis had come to his senses. Though the thought of giving Tarn a thrashing was still very much on his mind, he agreed with Cletus that they had to help their fellow desert dwellers. The brothers agreed: They had to get everyone out safely before the Pure Ones began their assault.

When Tavis was in the right frame of mind, he was a brilliant owl. The plan was his. They had two nights to carry it off. First, he and Cletus would begin a warning relay. The two of them would fly to the southern edge of the Broken Egg. They would tell the owls who lived in the outlying burrows that they must leave their homes immediately. Then those owls would fly or run north to warn two more owls each. Each little group of owls would hop from burrow to burrow, working their way north toward Tavis and Cletus's burrow. That way, not too many owls would be in the sky or on the ground at one time, and they would not arouse suspicion from any Pure Ones who might be keeping watch. They figured it wouldn't take them more than one night to get the word out to everyone. While the other owls were relaying the information, Tavis and Cletus would begin excavating. With their powerful talons, they reckoned they could dig through the earth pretty fast. They would dig a tunnel from their burrow to just beyond the earthen ridge of the Broken Egg's crater, near the border of Ambala. Then all the desert dwellers would escape through this tunnel and into the forest, hidden by the ridges from any aerial patrols, before the Pure Ones knew they were gone.

Neither Tavis nor Cletus wanted to think about what might happen if the plan went awry. Nor did they have the time. They had to act immediately for it all to work. They flew as fast as they could to deliver the first warnings. Then they returned to their burrow and began excavating. The plan was in motion.

Excavating was not as simple as the two Great Grays thought it would be. It looked easy enough when they watched Burrowing Owls do it, but it was hard work! They dug with all their might, and still it seemed they were just inching forward in the earth. As the night went on, a few of their Burrowing Owl neighbors showed up to help. Even then, progress was slower than either Tavis or Cletus expected. They excavated into the next day, and then into the next night.

Across the desert, two Burrowing Owls had just gotten the news that they would have to leave their home, or else.

"Should we really leave, Dill?" Jacy asked.

"I don't know, Jacy," Dill replied. "Odell sounded awfully scared. But he hadn't seen any of these Pure

Ones, just got the word from those two Great Grays who live up north."

"He said we had to leave tonight." Jacy bobbed her head nervously.

Jacy and Dill had been living in the desert for years, ever since the two became mates. Because leaving their home was a big decision, they decided that they needed to think about it and talk it over. They knew that they had to pass the warning on to their neighbors — that nice young couple sitting their eggs — but that would have to wait until they came to a decision. The two owls talked and talked; they just didn't know what to do. They were in such a tizzy, they didn't even notice the sound of digging coming from just beyond their burrow. Suddenly, the two Burrowing Owls were thrown off their feet. There was dirt and sand everywhere. The last thing that either owl saw before they died was the gray face of a Sooty Owl.

The sun had lit up the desert in a soft pink light. Tavis and Cletus emerged from the long tunnel they had been digging for the past two nights. Behind them the ridges of the Broken Egg rose into the sky. Across the desert to the north, a smear of dark marked the Forest Kingdom of Ambala. They had checked a few nights ago for signs of the Pure Ones in this area, and couldn't find any. They checked again. The coast was clear. The first of the desert dwellers began to exit the tunnel behind the brothers. One by one, the owls filed out of the tunnel, a little frazzled, but mostly relieved.

"We've done it!" Tavis said to Cletus, elated. "We've done it, brother!"

The two Great Grays rose straight into the air and did mirror-image spiral dives in celebration. They couldn't believe they pulled it off. They had discovered the Pure Ones' secret plan, formulated a plan of their own to save their neighbors, and carried it out without so much as a hiccup. They were proud of all their neighbors, too. They delivered the warning relay just as the brothers had hoped they would, and many of them helped by taking turns excavating. Cletus and Tavis bumped talons triumphantly.

As the last of the owls began to trickle out of the tunnel, Cletus and Tavis began to think about what to do next. They had to find a new home, obviously — all the owls did. Cletus reflected that it should be easy for him and Tavis. Being two grown owls, they could nest almost anywhere. But many of the Burrowing Owls from the desert had hatchlings, and that made finding safe, comfy nests all the more important. Cletus suddenly thought of something.

"Hey, Tavis?"

"Yes, brother?"

"Have you seen Saul and Trixie?"

Tavis looked at Cletus, dread growing in his eyes. "Not since a few days ago," he answered fretfully.

Cletus wilfed to what seemed like half his usual size. He hadn't seen them since the day he and Tavis met Tarn. They had not come through the tunnel. Saul and Trixie and all their eggs were still back in the desert. Either the warning relay was broken, or they just did not leave their burrow fast enough.

"Do you think . . . ?" Cletus couldn't bring himself to finish the question.

The brothers stared at each other for a long moment, trying to figure out what they should do. They had saved all the other owls from certain death, but their friends were left behind. There was a chance that they could not help them at all, a chance that Saul and Trixie were already dead. Should they risk their lives just for a chance to help them?

"I'm going back for them," Cletus said, and without waiting another moment, ducked his head into the tunnel.

"Not without me, you're not!" Tavis followed.

They didn't dare take to the sky, even though it would have brought them to Saul and Trixie's burrow faster. That dastardly Tarn knew them, and boldly flying into what was now the Pure Ones' territory would attract too much attention. The Pure Ones were sure to have guards keeping watch around the perimeter. So, the two Great Grays walked through the narrow tunnel as quickly as their legs would take them, which, for owls unaccustomed to walking, was rather slow.

They emerged in their old burrow at the end of the tunnel. Cletus peeked out carefully. It was midday and, as he expected, he didn't see any Pure Ones in the sky above. And they clearly hadn't breached their burrow underground. It was a short flight from here to Saul and Trixie's burrow, so the brothers decided they would fly low to the ground. They didn't have much of a choice; this wasn't the time to start digging new tunnels.

Cletus and Tavis quietly exited the burrow. As soon as they lifted off, they spotted trouble. Two Barn Owls appeared out of Tarn's burrow and headed straight for them. As they approached, more Pure Ones emerged from other burrows.

"Go on, Cletus! Go! I'll cover you!" Cletus heard Tavis shout.

He lowered his head and flapped his wings hard, driving himself toward Saul and Trixie's burrow. He saw Tavis dive and swipe at the two Barn Owls closest to them. Luckily, Tavis's enormous size made it an unfair fight. One after the other, the Barn Owls fell to the desert floor. Cletus didn't see how exactly Tavis dispatched the other oncoming Pure Ones; he left his brother to deal with them, and dove for Saul and Trixie's hollow. He spotted it easily because it was surrounded on three sides by some of the largest boulders in the desert.

Trixie sat atop her clutch of three eggs. The first should hatch any moment now, she could tell. It was an exciting time for their little family. Saul thought he had heard a ruckus outside earlier, and wondered what was going on. But he decided he would stay in his burrow today because he didn't want to miss the hatching of his first chick.

"Yee!" Trixie jumped up from her nest. "I think I just felt one move!" she exclaimed.

She and Saul leaned in to take a closer look at the eggs. They were concentrating so hard on them that they didn't notice when a big gray face poked into their burrow.

"Saul! Trixie! It's me, Cletus. Y'all in there?" Cletus asked with desperation in his voice.

The two Burrowing Owls almost jumped out of their feathers.

"Cletus!" Saul cried out. "You almost scared us half to death!"

"Well, half to death is better than all the way to death," Cletus quipped nervously, relieved to find his friends alive and well.

"What are you doing here?"

"The Pure Ones . . . we had a relay . . . the tunnel . . ." Cletus couldn't tell the story quickly enough. Finally, he just said, "No time, you all have to leave your burrow — for good. Come with me, right now!"

"WHAT?" Trixie was bewildered. "Our eggs are going to hatch any minute now, we can't leave!"

Cletus took a deep breath. "The Pure Ones are here. They've been building up their forces in the desert for Glaux knows how long now. They've built a massive system of burrows and underground tunnels. They're killing all the owls who live here. They've already killed Hiram, and Glaux knows who else. If you want to live, you have to come with me!"

"Our eggs!" Trixie said helplessly. She had wilfed to the size of a mouse as she listened to Cletus.

"You have to leave *for* your eggs!"

The Burrowing Owl pair nodded to each other, and then to Cletus.

"Quickly. I'll help you with your eggs. The Pure Ones are out there. We will hold them off. You must flee as best you can. Run or fly! Head for our burrow, there's a tunnel that will lead you to the northern edge of the desert. Once you're in the tunnel, run and don't look back," Cletus instructed.

Just then, Tavis arrived at the burrow with splatters of blood in his feathers.

"I took care of them. I didn't let any of 'em get back to call for reinforcements," Tavis said proudly. "These boulders here may have saved your lives!" he added.

It was true, Cletus realized. The boulders that surrounded Saul and Trixie's burrow kept the Pure Ones from digging through. They were lucky. But it wasn't going to keep them safe forever.

Saul and Trixie each picked up an egg from the nest and headed out of the burrow. Cletus reached a foot into the nest. The white orb seemed so tiny and fragile in the talons of the Great Gray that it made the usually nimble Cletus feel like a clumsy giant.

But before he could pick it up, the last egg wobbled and cracked, right in front of Cletus's eyes. He stared in amazement — he had never seen a chick hatch before. And although he always imagined it to be unremarkable, he was enthralled by the simple process. The tiny chick inside the egg stretched and pushed aside the pieces of the shell that housed it. And immediately it seemed impossible that it had fit into the little egg from which it hatched just a moment ago. The chick plopped into the nest, squirming.

"Trixie! Saul!" Cletus finally managed to find his voice and call out. He backed away from the nest to let the new parents see their chick.

Trixie and Saul rushed to their newly hatched chick. For just a moment, Cletus saw utter joy and awe in their eyes. Their look of joy was quickly replaced by a look of worry.

"What do we do now?" asked Saul.

At the same time, Tavis spotted trouble in the air. "Incoming! Barn Owls from the east. Three of them."

"Put the chick on my back," Cletus instructed. "I'll keep it safe, I promise. You stick to the plan and fly as fast as you can."

Cletus knew that the best chance the tiny new chick had was as his passenger. Trixie and Saul knew it, too. With great care, they picked up the tiny chick and placed it on Cletus's back, right between the wings. They grabbed the remaining two eggs and lifted off after Tavis.

Cletus took to the air. He realized immediately that he could not fly in his usual way. He had to balance the chick in the middle of his back — this meant no banking, no rolling, and definitely no fancy midair talon work. This might have been okay if he were merely trying to get from one place to another, but it just wouldn't do right now.

The Pure Ones were on them as soon as the two Great Grays and now three Burrowing Owls began their flight. The burrow, which was only a short flight away, seemed like it was on the other side of the world. Between them and their goal were four Sooty Owls and two Barn Owls.

Tavis flew point and met the six attackers head-on. He was a flash of whirling, darting gray feathers.

> *My desert, my home,*
> *You better leave us alone!*
> *This is my sky, you hear?*
> *The brothers gray you ought to fear.*
> *Pure this, pure that,*
> *I'll see you go splat!*

Two of the Sooties fell within a heartbeat. Tavis charged after another.

One of the Barn Owls was on top of Saul. Saul was not the strongest flier to begin with, and clutching an egg in his talons made it worse. He could barely defend himself. He tried to get away, but the remaining Sooties now surrounded him. Tavis was at his side as soon as he saw that his friend was in trouble.

"YA!" He dove into the fray with a battle cry. Before anyone could blink, Tavis was talon to talon with the Barn Owl who went after Saul. Tavis slashed at the owl and caught him at the base of the wing. The owl spun out of control and fell to the ground below.

In the meantime, the two Sooties swiped at Saul and Trixie. It was a despicable move — attacking the smallest owls, who were carrying eggs — but that was what the Pure Ones did. One of the Sooties grazed Saul on the tail. It wasn't enough to hurt him but it made him lose his balance as well as his hold on the egg. The egg fell toward the ground. Cletus's yellow eyes zoomed in on the tiny white egg. He dove for it as soon as he saw it leave Saul's clutch. Just before it hit the ground, Cletus caught it with his right talons.

He would have been relieved, except that the chick on his back slid to one side during the maneuver. As he began to tip in the opposite direction to center his little passenger, a Sooty Owl came within a wingspan of him. Cletus looked for Tavis. He was pytes away, battling the other Sooty. Saul had recovered, but he and Trixie were still trying to outfly the last Barn Owl. The Sooty Owl knew that Cletus was near helpless and dove at him. Cletus banked ever so slightly to avoid him, and the chick on his back slipped again. This time, it almost slid off of Cletus's back entirely. As he felt the chick slide, Cletus thought his gizzard would jump out of his beak. The Sooty Owl attacked again, and this time, he went after the tiny Burrowing Owl chick on the Great Gray's back.

Tavis dispatched his Sooty attacker with ease. He looked toward his brother and gasped in horror. He was going to lose the chick! Tavis flapped his wings hard and drove himself toward the last Sooty Owl. But before he could reach him, Trixie was there. With one foot firmly clutching an egg, Trixie dove toward the Sooty. The Sooty expected the smaller owl to try to fly away, not to counterattack. Trixie drove her razor-sharp beak into the Sooty Owl's eye. There was a sickening little *pop*. The Sooty screamed and went yeep.

They were but a few wing beats away from the tunnel now and of their attackers only the Barn Owl remained, and she was retreating. Cletus straightened himself in flight and returned the chick to the center of his back. They were all about to breathe a sigh of relief when Tavis turned and saw scores of Pure Ones on the horizon. Worse, Tarn and two of his Burrowing Owl minions had emerged from his burrow.

"The tunnel! NOW!" he yelled.

The four owls dove for the opening of the burrow. Saul and Trixie went in first and ran for the tunnel. Cletus went in next, with the chick and the egg. When he was safely in the tunnel, he gently slid the hatchling off his back and returned it to its parents.

Tavis was the last into the tunnel. Immediately, Tarn and the two Burrowing Owls went into the tunnel after them.

"If it isn't my least favorite neighbors," Tarn said. "I should have known you'd be a problem."

"Tarn, you bad-butt owl . . ." Tavis said as he tried to slash at him. It was near impossible as the tunnel was far too small for a Great Gray to fight in.

Tarn knew this. Each time Tavis attacked, Tarn jumped back out of the way. And each time Tavis pulled his talons back to regain his balance, Tarn lashed out at the Great Gray. None of them were death blows, but Tarn was relentless. Tavis was hurt. The cuts on his chest and legs burned, but his hatred of this Burrowing Owl burned hotter. He tried over and over to get one good swipe at Tarn, but each time, Tarn was just out of reach.

Cletus saw what was happening. "Tavis, stop fighting, you can't win in here!" Cletus yelled from a little farther in the tunnel. "It's time to run!"

"No! We can't let him get away with this!" Tavis grunted.

Tarn churred tauntingly.

"Remember your plan, Tavis. It's time to go!" Cletus yelled again.

Tavis had almost forgotten all about this part of the plan. He was near delirious with battle fever. He wanted so badly to kill this owl — this owl who turned on his fellow Burrowing Owls to join the Pure Ones, this owl who masterminded the takeover of all the burrows, this owl who sought to kill him and all his neighbors in the Desert of Kuneer.

There was a great kerfuffle outside the tunnel. The rest of the Pure Ones had arrived. Enemy owls were filling the tunnel.

"Let's go, Tavis," Cletus said again. He knew that his brother was loath to turn away from this fight. But if Tavis didn't turn away now, all would be lost. "We came back for Saul and Trixie and their eggs. We can't fail them now. Think of that little chick back there."

Tavis knew his brother was right this time. The only way he could win the fight was to run away. With Tarn still slashing and pecking at him, Tavis turned his back and ran as fast as he could into the tunnel. When he got to the spot that he had marked earlier with two gray feathers, he shouted, "Fail-safe!"

It was the last part of Tavis's plan. He had thought that the Pure Ones would likely follow the desert dwellers into the tunnel and try to stop them from leaving. So when he and Cletus dug the tunnel, they built in an extra feature. Tavis reached up with his beak and gave a good tug at the tumbleweed branch that stuck out of the roof of the tunnel. The tumbleweed, along with rocks and sand, fell into the tunnel and blocked it completely from the Pure Ones on the other side. The tunnel was suddenly filled with silence.

The two Great Grays and the family of Burrowing Owls emerged into the twilight at the northeastern edge of the Desert of Kuneer. They were all tired and dirty, but they were alive. The two eggs had not a scratch on them, and the newly hatched chick was sleeping peacefully. Tavis's wounds still burned, but they would heal.

"You saved our family," Trixie said to the brothers. "We can't thank you enough."

"We've decided to call this young'un 'Gray,' for his Great Gray saviors," Saul added.

"I think that's a fine name," Cletus replied. Tavis nodded in agreement.

From where they stood, the brothers could see the stands of tall trees in the Forest Kingdom of Ambala in the distance. They had run away from Ambala all those years ago in part to get away from the Pure Ones. Now, here they were, once again homeless because of the Pure Ones. But there was one big difference. This time they were saviors. This time they had not let themselves or others be bullied by the Pure Ones. They prevented other owlets from being orphaned, as they had been. And they kept families together.

Here at the great tree, Tavis and Cletus have found their permanent home and been reunited with their long-lost brother, Twilight. Their astonishing desert rescue is being taught to young owls in the search-and-rescue chaw so others may be saved. These brave brothers have exemplified ingenuity, courage, teamwork, and coolheadedness in the heat of battle. And perhaps most important, they've taught us that sometimes victory is found in retreat.

FIVE

A Secret in Braithe's Gizzard

Of the great tree's many friends, I can think of few as intriguing as the Whiskered Screech, Braithe, the founder of the Brad, the Place of Living Books in the forests of Ambala. There, every owl who loves to read becomes a book — memorizing every word on every page until he or she is able to recite the entire work at will. As if that were not enough, Braithe, along with the rest of the Greenowls of Ambala, bravely flew to the aid of the Band and the great tree in the Battle of Balefire Night. The Guardians and the Greenowls came together to defeat the Blue Brigade and the Striga.

Braithe's story is one of self-discovery. It was shortly after that fateful Balefire Night that the truth began to unfold. With the help of friends in this world and beyond, Braithe uncovered clues that helped him to solve a mystery that had plagued him since his fledgling days. I was touched that Braithe chose to share his story with me, and then allowed me to share it with you.

It was near dawn. Braithe flew silently over the Forest of Ambala. He had just visited the library at the Great Ga'Hoole Tree again, and had found several volumes of poetry that he wanted to commit to memory. He carried one of them in his botkin now. He would have much work to do in the Brad in the coming nights. Braithe looked for the distinctive rounded crowns of the heartwood trees that marked its presence and banked toward home.

The entire kingdom of Ambala was verdant. But the Brad, the place Braithe called home, was especially lush. The Brad was hidden in a valley so densely covered with thick moss that it was known as a moss hole. The grove of heartwood trees that Braithe flew toward grew to enormous heights there, and hid the valley's great depth from above. Unsuspecting birds overflying the Brad would never guess there was such a drop in the land below.

As he spiraled downward into the dell, the early morning light changed from bright and clear rays to a dim and dreamy green glow. Some have compared the Brad to the spirit woods. True, there was something not quite real about this place, but Braithe never thought of it as eerie as he did the spirit woods west of the Island of Hoole. He had visited the spirit woods just once before, having been drawn to it for no particular reason he could name. In the short time he was there, he heard voices in the wind and saw strange reflections in the mist. He found it cold and disquieting, even though he didn't really believe in scrooms, and left as quickly as he had come. This place, the Brad, on the other wing, was a place of enchantment. And more important, it was home — it felt welcoming and comforting.

Just as he was landing on a mossy rock, an owl — an old, grizzled Whiskered Screech — floated slowly by Braithe. *Funny*, he thought, *the owl is silent.* In the Brad, owls were constantly talking, reciting the words found in all the books that they were able to collect. If it was not for the thick moss covering every surface, the valley would be reverberating with the hoots of owls, and snatches of prose and verse. Braithe knew every owl in the dell and looked around to see who had just wafted by. Only silence and stillness greeted him. He seemed to be alone in this part of the Brad. He noted to himself that he should find out who that owl was. He always made it a point to keep track of everyone here, like a living catalog. But it would have to wait until night; now it was time for a well-deserved rest.

Braithe nestled down into the soft moss in the hollow of a heartwood. His hollow was close to the ground. The heartwood's immense size and the valley's great depth meant that even during the day, the hollow was in near darkness. Owls who did not live in the Brad often had trouble falling asleep in such conditions, but Braithe was used to it. His head was heavy and he drifted off to sleep and immediately into the midst of a deep and vivid dream. . . .

Braithe was flying as fast as he could over a large stretch of water on a moonless night. He turned to look back. Something was following him. No, something was *chasing* him. He turned and searched the sky again. He saw no one, yet he knew he was being pursued. He flapped his wings harder, lifting himself higher. Thunder rumbled above him in a low, menacing groan. *I'll be safer down low, closer to the water.* He dove toward its surface. He turned again. And again, he saw no one. But he felt a presence and he knew his pursuer was getting closer. Suddenly, he heard a long, feather-raising screech. It reverberated off the surface of the water. *No, it came from the water.*

He looked down into the still, black surface. Lightning lit up the sky, and Braithe saw his own reflection. It glided along with him, wing beat for wing beat. As he watched, his reflection began to grow older and turned into that of his da, Bo. Braithe's father had disappeared shortly after Braithe was fully fledged. Braithe never knew what happened to him, and it always pecked at the back of his gizzard. His disappearance wasn't the only thing about his da that haunted him. The reflection of Bo stared up at Braithe from the surface of the dark water. His beak opened, but no sound came out.

As Braithe flew, the reflection changed again, growing older still. Its feathers began to thin and lose their color. Its eyes grew dull. Its beak lost its luster, and marks — no, scars — appeared on it. If this was truly him, he was aging, withering in front of his very own eyes. The reflection opened its beak again. This time, it let out a chilling, low growl.

"Lil's spots," it said.

Braithe didn't understand.

The voice grew louder and more insistent. "Lil's spots! Lil's spots!" it screamed.

Braithe suddenly felt as if he was being pulled toward the water. He was falling, plunging into his own reflection. He tried to flap his wings but the water made them heavy — too heavy to move. He reached out with his talons in a futile attempt to hold on to something, but they, too, were leaden. He tried to cry out, but no sound came out of his beak. The two owls, one real and one reflected, became one in the darkness of the water.

"LIL'S SPOTS!" Braithe woke up shouting.

He took several shallow breaths before he realized that he was safely nestled in his hollow. He looked down and saw that he had unknowingly puffed out his feathers in a threat display. His heart was racing and his gizzard felt like a rock. He peeked out of his hollow. The sun was still high in the sky, so he could not have been asleep for long. Braithe settled back down and tried to fall asleep, but sleep would not come.

The dreams are back, he thought woefully. Ever since his father disappeared, Braithe had been haunted by dreams of him. Most often in these dreams, he would encounter his da somewhere familiar, but his da would not recognize him. Sometimes he dreamed that he was watching his da go yeep from a perch very high up, helpless to save him. The dream he'd just had of his reflection in the water was a new one, and it was every bit as disturbing as the others. For many moon cycles now, Braithe thought he was free of these dreams. All the activity recently — meeting Soren and the other Guardians of Ga'Hoole, helping the Guardians in their battles against the Blue Brigade and the Pure Ones, and discovering new libraries — had kept his mind busy and driven the dreams away. But now, as things quieted down again, the dreams were making their return. They would rob him of sleep, Braithe knew, and make his waking hours miserable.

Braithe reached with a talon into what looked like a knot in the heartwood, opening a tiny, hidden compartment behind the knot. He pulled out a small pouch. He hadn't looked at its contents since last autumn, when the crowns of the heartwoods were a fiery shade of red. He reached between the layers of worn lemming leather and pulled out several fragments of a parchment.

He had found the fragments in his mum's nest after she had died of gray scale two summers ago. The first time he had read the parchment, he was confused. Then, as he digested what he read, his confusion turned into devastation. It was his da's writing; he recognized it easily. The letter had been written to his mum. It mentioned things, puzzling and alarming things, that Braithe wanted desperately to make sense of, but never could. He knew every word written on those fragments, they were seared into his memory, but he read them again.

My work at St. Aggie's is going well. . . . my devotion to Skench and Sporn . . . am most loyal to St. Aggie's . . . be more aggressive on raids . . . We are preparing to raid nests in the Forest Kingdom of Tyto. . . . deliver the next egg to them . . . that the last egg I snatched from . . . happy to raise it as my own . . .

St. Aggie's was the despicable group of owls who owl-napped hatchlings and eggs from their nests, who moon blinked them to make them docile and unquestioning, who made the owl families of Ambala live in a constant state of fear, season after season. Braithe grew up hearing stories of their villainy and was no stranger to the evil deeds of Skench and her cohorts. He also heard myriad stories of a Spotted Owl named Hortense, who bravely infiltrated St. Aggie's to rescue countless eggs. Braithe had heard the saying all his life: "A hero is known by only one name, and that name is Hortense." Ambala never took for granted the sacrifice made by Hortense, nor did it ever forgive the atrocities committed by the owls of St. Aggie's.

How was it possible that Braithe's own father was working for St. Aggie's, as the fragments of parchment implied? Over and over Braithe reviewed the damning letter for clues: *My work at St. Aggie's is going well. . . .* That certainly sounded bad. *The last egg I snatched . . .* Was his da really an egg snatcher? *Happy to raise it as my own . . .* Could Braithe himself have hatched from a snatched egg? Was Bo not even his real da? And why had his mum never spoken of this? Did she know of her mate's treachery all along? The letter must have meant a great deal to her if she kept its fragments. Now it was too late to ask either of them. Braithe feared that he would never find the answers.

He read the fragments again. Each time he looked at the words, he hoped he would discover something, a new tidbit of information, a revelation he had previously missed. But the words were the same, as were the pieces of soft, worn parchment. Same, too, was the potent mix of shame and doubt gnawing at his gizzard. *My father, an egg snatcher working for St. Aggie's! How can it be true?*

Braithe carefully tucked the parchment back into the leather pouch. He took out one of the books of poetry he had brought back from the great tree and began to read. He knew sleep would elude him today.

A few nights later, Braithe found himself perched in a heartwood in front of three eager owlets. It was story time for the family of young Spotted Owls. Sasha, Patch, and Avi were very excited because they were about to hear one of their favorite tales from the Others: "The Ransom of Red Chief." And Braithe was one of their favorite storytellers in all of the Brad.

"It looked like a good thing: but wait till I tell you . . ." Braithe began.

"The Ransom of Red Chief" was a simple tale written by O. Henry, one of the Others. In it, two criminals kidnap a little boy for ransom. But their young captive, a bratty and mischievous boy who calls himself Red Chief, actually enjoys staying with his kidnappers, thinking it a great adventure. Red Chief drives his captors yoicks with his game of pretend, tormenting them with pranks and making them play wearying games with him. In the end, instead of getting the ransom they demanded, the two criminals pay the boy's father to take him back.

Sasha, Patch, and Avi had heard the story so many times that they nearly had it memorized themselves. Still, they listened with great anticipation.

Braithe got to the part where the two criminals first take the boy captive. He recited: "'That boy put up a fight like a welterweight cinnamon bear; but, at last, we got him down in the bottom of the buggy and drove away.'" His mind began to wander. *The Others snatched young'uns, too,* he thought. *How terrible.* He began to think about his da again, and all the owlets and eggs he might have snatched from families who *did* want them back. And if he was hatched from a snatched egg, who were his real parents, and did *they* want him back?

The three owlets listening to Braithe tilted their heads and then looked at one another quizzically. He wasn't telling the story right. Not only that, Braithe's voice had become monotonous to the point of being too boring to listen to. It was a far cry from the animated and exciting storytelling they were used to.

Braithe finished the story, all the while still thinking of his father, Bo, St. Aggie's, and the snatched eggs. He looked up at the three owlets. They stared at him curiously.

"Um, I think you missed a part," said Avi.

"You missed the *best* part!" complained Patch.

"Yeah, you got the ending all wrong! Without the part about the dad's letter, it doesn't even make sense!" added Sasha.

Braithe was confused. He thought he had told the whole story just as it was written.

The owlets were quick to point out his mistake.

"The dad sends a letter back to the bad guys, he says no, I won't give you two thousand dollars and if you want me to take Red Chief back, you're going to have to give *me* money!" Sasha exclaimed in a single breath.

"And when they bring Red Chief back the dad has to hold on to him because he doesn't want to go home and keeps trying to run back to Bill and Sam. . . ."

"And *then* the two criminals run away!" Avi finished for his brother.

"I missed all of that?" asked Braithe, embarrassed by his own blunder.

"YES!" the three owlets whined, looking disappointed.

Patch added, "It's a good thing we already knew the story. If we had never heard it before, we might have thought it was a bad story. But it's a good story, a really good one."

"I'm very sorry," said Braithe, and he was. He felt he had let the owlets down. He couldn't believe that he would miss something so simple yet so vital to the story.

"It's okay," said Sasha, "just please remember the whole story next time."

Braithe roosted in his nest, determined to sleep. He had not slept in days. His eyes were heavy and he felt groggy, but every time he began to doze, he started himself awake. It was a vicious cycle — the less he slept, the more he worried about not sleeping. It was beginning to make him forget things. Just the other night, Braithe had to stop midway through reciting the Fire Cycle of the legends to another group of hatchlings. He had forgotten the story! *The Fire Cycle, of all things, for shame!* Getting lost while reciting a story by one of the Others was one thing, but the Fire Cycle was different. It was one of the first tales he had ever memorized, one that parents have told to their owlets for generations, one that he thought was etched in the deepest part of his memory. The dreams of his father were tormenting him more than he had realized. They were beginning to cause him to lose that which was most precious to him — the books he kept in his mind. Even when he was awake, his thoughts kept returning to his da and the fragments of parchment hidden in the secret compartment in the knot. Braithe wondered if he could ever be free of his haunting dreams.

As he nestled deeper into the moss, he noticed that a stillness had fallen over the dell. It was as if a heavy cloud had enveloped him. The air thickened and blurred with mist. Braithe felt as if he were in a dream, but he knew he was still wide awake. From the corner of his eye, Braithe saw an owl. His head felt almost too heavy to move. He had to will himself to turn his head toward the direction of the owl. But when he did, he saw nothing but the forest around him.

Braithe stared into the mist. Then, slowly, the

lingering mist began to gather itself into the shape of an owl. The image was shimmering and shifting in the dim light but it was now clearly an old Whiskered Screech. Braithe saw that the owl was not just old, he was decrepit and battered. He was missing a toe on his left foot, his left eye seemed to be stuck in a perpetual squint, and his beak had a deep notch in it. Braithe realized then that the owl was the reflection he had seen in his dream. He should have been scared, but he wasn't. He looked at the old owl with searching eyes. Despite his ghastly appearance, there was something oddly comforting and familiar about him.

The old Whiskered Screech moved his beak as if to say something. The sound that Braithe heard reminded him of distant thunder. Braithe tried to lean toward the owl to hear better. Suddenly, he felt himself rising from his nest, yet he knew he was perfectly still. Braithe watched as a misty version of himself drifted toward the old owl.

The two mist owls hovered outside of Braithe's hollow.

What is happening? Who are you? Braithe asked the apparition. He wasn't using his voice, he realized, and he wasn't using his body, either. He had left his body behind on the nest, and a misty version of himself was speaking to the old Whiskered Screech — using only his mind — and the old owl heard him.

But instead of answering his questions, the old owl gazed at him wistfully and said again, *Lil's spots*, just as Braithe had heard in his dream.

I don't understand. Are you a scroom?

I'm Ezylryb. Or Lyze of Kiel, as I was once called.

The weather ryb from the great tree? I've heard of you, of course! But why are you here?

Your gizzard is troubled. You carry a great burden ... a secret that fills you with shame. Your da ...

What do you know about my da? Braithe thought desperately. This scroom was reading his gizzard as well as his mind!

Your da was a good owl.

These fragments of parchment ... Braithe looked back at his nest. Thoughts rushed from him. In his mind he explained to Ezylryb about the fragments of the letter that he had found, and how he suspected that his da had been in league with the owls of St. Aggie's, and was an egg snatcher. He also told him about his fears of having been snatched himself as an egg. When he was finished, the misty Ezylryb looked at him with a strange mix of doubt and tenderness.

Your da was a good owl, the scroom repeated.

Braithe wanted desperately to believe the old scroom.

Then what does this letter mean? Why does it say that my da was loyal to St. Aggie's? Why does it say that he snatched eggs?

I don't know, lad, I don't know. . . . Ezylryb's misty image began to fade.

Wait! Then why are you here? Braithe asked. *Isn't it true that scrooms always have unfinished business? Do you think this is yours?*

Ezylryb's scroom said nothing for what seemed to Braithe like an eternity. Finally, he responded. *Something drew me here. I had visited Ambala many times in my life, but never knew about this place. Then, after passing, I found myself here again and again, and I didn't know why. That is, until I saw you. I think I needed to see you. And maybe you also needed to see me. To know where you came from and who you are.*

Braithe was at a loss for words. He knew where he came from — Ambala — but that his da was a good owl he couldn't quite believe, much as he wanted to. Sadness possessed him again.

I guess I thought you would know. I wish you could tell me more. I wish you had all the answers. And more than anything I wish I could believe that my da was a good owl. What he wrote on that parchment seems to prove otherwise, Braithe replied.

When I passed, I found I knew many things. But not every-thing. It's like I know the story, but not all the words that make up the story. I know he was good, though not why, or how.

Braithe pondered this. *If he was a good owl, then what was he doing at St. . . .* Braithe paused midthought. He was about to ask a rhetorical question when something that Ezylryb said hit him. *The story!* He was reminded of his telling of "The Ransom of Red Chief" to the three Spotted Owlets a few nights ago. He thought he was tell-ing the story, but he'd left out some of the words. *And a few missing words can change a story completely!* Maybe he'd got his da's story all wrong.

He was a good owl at St. Aggie's, Braithe continued. *Of course, there were good owls at St. Aggie's! Hortense! All those stories I've heard about how Hortense saved hundreds of eggs and owlets while pretending to be moon blinked. And Grimble. Soren has told me about the noble Grimble, who helped him and Gylfie to escape. If only I could have spoken to one of them. . . .*

Hortense is Mist, said Ezylryb's scroom.

I know, thought Braithe sadly. *Hortense is gone, into the mists of time, long gone. . . .*

No. Hortense is Mist. Her name is Mist.

Braithe's mind was racing, as was his gizzard. *What?!* he thought.

She is no longer known as Hortense, but she lives, here, in Ambala. You know her as Mist.

Mist! Braithe repeated. He could hardly believe it. He knew Mist well. But he never knew that she was once the celebrated Hortense. The answers to his questions might have been a night's flight away all along. He just didn't know to ask. As he pondered this, the mist surrounding him began to dissolve and Ezylryb faded away.

When night fell, Braithe flew north to the place of eagles and flying snakes with the fragments of parchment clutched in his talons. There he found the scintillating and vaporous owl he had always known as Mist, and her two companions, the eagles Zan and Streak.

What Braithe learned was that, as Hortense, Mist hadn't known Braithe's father, Bo. After she was thrown off the highest cliff at St. Aggie's and caught by Streak, her career as an infiltrator ended, and she returned to Ambala. As she recuperated, she had gotten word that a Whiskered Screech had taken her place as a slipgizzle at St. Aggie's. The owl worked tirelessly and rescued scores of eggs and chicks with the help of the eagles Streak and Zan, just as Hortense had done. But they never knew his real name. He was known only by his code name: 16-7. "I'm not doing this to be a hero," he had told them. "I'm doing this for the future of Ambala."

When Zan saw the fragments of parchment that Braithe held, she immediately went to her nest and brought back a small botkin. She dug through the botkin and pulled out a few more fragments of parchment.

"We saved all the letters we ever received from 16-7 — from Bo, I mean," Streak explained. "These fragments were brought to us by his mate . . . your mother, I presume. She did not want to keep anything in her nest that implicated her mate as a slipgizzle in case the nest was ever raided by St. Aggie's."

"Why do you suppose she kept these fragments, then?" asked Braithe.

"I don't know," answered Streak.

Zan looked at Streak and opened her beak to signal something. Streak nodded, and said, "Zan thinks your mum must have wanted to hold on to something from your da, something to remember him by. But she couldn't keep the whole letter because it implicated him. So, she tore away the parts that did and kept the rest."

Braithe look the fragments of the parchment from Zan. He laid them on the wide branch on which he perched, and pieced them together with the fragments he brought. Finally, he had the whole letter before him, and it told the whole story:

> My Dearest,
>
> My work at St. Aggie's is going well. However, I fear that some owls here are beginning to question my devotion to Skench and Sporn. I must redouble my efforts to convince them that I am most loyal to St. Aggie's. I'm afraid that means I'll have to be more aggressive on raids.
>
> We are preparing to raid nests in the Forest Kingdom of Tyto again. I've already told Streak and Zan that I'll be ready to deliver the next egg to them on the new moon. In my last conversation with the eagles, I was told that the last egg I snatched from the eggorium never hatched. That is sad news indeed, for I would have been happy to raise it as my own. I suspect our son would have loved a little brother or sister.
>
> I know my work has been hard on our family, especially on young Braithe, but I feel that it is vital to Ambala and to owlkind that I continue. The tyrants of St. Aggie's must be stopped at all costs. Ambala must resist. I hope to return to you soon.
>
> Yours always,
>
> 16-7

Braithe sighed deeply. He needed no scroom to tell him now that his da was a good and noble owl. He had the proof before him. He felt his gizzard untwist and a weight lift from his broad breast. He packed all the fragments of the restored letter into a small botkin and thanked Zan and Streak for their revelations. He bid farewell to Mist. She seemed to shimmer with gladness as he took to the air. Banking, swooping, and playing on the thermals, he winged it home to the Brad. He felt his life was beginning anew and was full of wonderful possibilities. The wind was a caress, and the stars were not twinkling but smiling down on him.

Back at the Brad, Braithe settled into his nest and drifted off into a deep, restful, dreamless sleep. Near the end of the day, at first dark he awoke to the odd sensation that he was being watched. There, just a wingspan from his nest, the scroom of Ezylryb coalesced out of the early evening fog that hung in the dell. The old owl seemed to stare at Braithe.

You! Back again? Braithe exclaimed. *I thought your work was done. But I am glad, so glad! I wanted to thank you.* The thoughts tumbled from Braithe's mind toward the old Whiskered Screech. The scroom seemed to churr in answer.

Lil's spots.

Lil's spots? Braithe repeated.

Yes, Lil's spots.

The voice Braithe heard in his head was soft and slightly melancholy, but in it Braithe also sensed contentment and relief. *You have inherited her spots,* Ezylryb went on. *Those mahogany and white spots on your wings . . . Mahogany and white, your da had the same spots on his wings. They came from his mother — my mate. Lil.*

Inherited? Braithe asked with his mind's voice. *I don't understand.*

Nor did I, until I passed. I thought I had lost the egg, my last connection to my Lil, during the battle of the Ice Claws. But that egg hatched. And that chick survived.

Braithe was puzzled. What had all of this to do with him? And why had Ezylryb spoken of inheritance? The scroom was beginning to fade before him.

Wait! he called to Ezylryb with his mind.

You say you know you come from Ambala, lad, but it's a little more complicated than that. Our chick, mine and Lil's, was not lost. Good-hearted owls found him, took him to Ambala, and raised him as their own. Ezylryb's image seemed to solidify momentarily, and his chest to swell with pride. *They named him Bo! He lived a good life as a good owl.*

Braithe tried to make sense of what he just heard. He stared at the scroom of Ezylryb in disbelief.

How do you know all this?

When I passed from this world it came to me little by little until I just knew. Then it was as if I had always known.

Braithe understood, at last. *But this means —*

Bo was my son, Ezylryb intoned in Braithe's mind. *And he was your father, so —*

You are my grandda!

Indeed, the scroom answered softly. *Now and forever . . .*

Then the scroom of Ezylryb faded and was gone.

Braithe sat silent in his nest while the night grew full and dark around him. The scroom was truly gone, Braithe could feel it. And yet Ezylryb remained — in Braithe's veins and sinews, in his gizzard and his heart. The young Greenowl of Ambala spread his wings and rose into the deep blue-emerald air of the Brad. He soared up, up, up into the open sky above its mighty heartwoods and set his course for the Great Ga'Hoole Tree. He had much to ask Soren about his grandfather.

All of us who know Braithe have seen a deep and subtle change in him these last several moon cycles. His voice rings with a new lightness, there is fresh power and spring in the great sweep of his wings, and according to the young owls under his tutelage in the Brad, he never forgets any of the words in his stories anymore. I think, dear reader, we know the reason for this happy change!

SIX

Cleve's Sorrow

How does one begin to write about someone so ... *close. Literally! How does one write about someone who is reading at the other end of the hollow as my quill scribbles across this page. I speak, of course, of my dear Cleve. I want to tell you his tale, for I think it's one worth telling, but I do not think I could do justice to it. I think, instead, I will ask Cleve to tell his own tale. It seems only fair, as he, too, is a great scholar and an accomplished writer.*

Cleve, dear, the page is yours. Tell your story as only you can.

Why, I'm honored, Otuli —

Wait! *I will need to retain editing privileges, of course. All right, now, the page is yours.*

Thank you, Otulissa, I'm honored that you think so highly of my story and my —

Please, Cleve, address the readers, we have to remember the readers here.

Oh. Of course. I am Cleve of Firthmore. I hail from Firthmore Passage in the Tridents of the Northern

Kingdoms. I am a student of the healing arts, who has spent many seasons cloistered at the Glauxian retreat on the island in the Bitter Sea. I came to the Great Ga'Hoole Tree in —

They know all that, my dear. I was thinking you'd talk about what happened before that. What about your clan? Don't forget to talk about your ancestors, it's important, you know, for posterity.

So the page is mine, you say?

Yes. But the book is still mine, and I will get the final word.

All right then. I guess I can say a few words about my clan. Mine is called the Clan of Krakor, one of the most ancient in the Northern Kingdoms. The Krakish language was named for it. In fact, the clan is known for its rich history and colorful lore. Many writers, poets, and historians have come out of my clan.

Like the great Strix Emerilla, the renowned weathertrix of the last century.

Yes, I was getting to that, but now I don't have to.

Oh, and you're a prince, don't forget that.

Otulissa, may I begin?

Oh, of course. That was my last interruption, I promise.

The story I tell is a sad one, one that I have carried in my heart and gizzard all my life. It's about my brother, Clay, may Glaux keep his soul. Many have wondered why I have renounced violence and war. Now, you'll learn the reason.

My brother, Clay, short for Claymore, was hatched moments before I was. In old northern families like ours, hatch order was very important. The first hatched would be named the rightful heir, and claim titles and ownership of hollows. In my family, the heir also inherited a collection of rare and ancient weapons that served as important symbols of our clan's accomplishments in the earliest ages of the Northern Kingdoms.

Among these was a pair of battle claws called Unguis Montania, or Mountain Claws in Hoolian. It's one of two pairs of ancient battle claws that belonged to the Clan of Krakor. The Unguis Oceania was the other, but those did not belong to the Hollow of Snarth. Those belonged to some distant cousins of ours who had a hollow on the other side of Firthmore, the Hollow of Kyran. The two pairs of battle claws were forged a long time ago by two brothers from our clan. They had been through many historic battles. And even though they would be practically useless in combat up against modern battle claws, they were passed from generation to generation in Firthmore. They were very valuable to our clan.

There was a saying among the aristocratic clans in the Northern Kingdoms: Each family had to have an "heir and a spare." So there was Claymore, egg tooth at the ready, hatching only seconds before I did. The ancient Mountain Claws were ceremoniously brought into the hollow nights before the hatching. And it was under the gleam of those battle claws that Claymore was hatched. Clay was the heir. I, the second to hatch, was just the spare.

As with all the firstborns in our part of the world, certain expectations were placed on Clay from a very young age. He was supposed to be strong in body and in spirit, and smart in academics and in life. He was to be trained to become a great warrior as well as an able leader. Da had an entire staff of reputable owls to ensure his son's success — a master of arms, a flight instructor, a master of the hunt, a political strategist, tutors in every subject, you name it. There was even a young squire whose sole task was to keep the Mountain Claws polished for Clay. Jak was his name: I'll never forget Jak. Jak was just a fledgling when he became our squire. He was from a common family, who thought it a great honor to send their son to the Hollow of Snarth as a squire. He saw Clay and me as big brothers, I suppose. He followed us around everywhere, and copied everything we did. One time, I even found him trying on my practice battle claws.

Mum and Da's expectations of me were never that high. As the "spare," I supposed I really could have led a life of leisure if I had wanted. Da thought it best for Clay, however, that I be brought up by his side, to provide a bit of brotherly competition. But Clay was always small for his age, and had trouble with all those Firsts. I was younger, but I was bigger and stronger. Early on, we had some of our First ceremonies on the same night, but by the time we reached First Flight, I had mine long before he had his. Those of you who know my reputation as a pacifist might be surprised to know that I was the first to wear battle claws and the first to wield an ice sword.

You know that I am *not* a fighting owl. I practiced with weapons as a young'un, sure, but I never fought in a real battle. The Northern Kingdoms were always entrenched in warfare. The military tradition there is strong even to this day. Clay and I were practically hatched with ice daggers in our talons. Weapons were both practical and symbolic to my clan. Why, it was even a family custom to bring the Mountain Claws to every one of our First ceremonies so that Da could tap us lightly on the wings with it when we completed our tasks. Jak kept them polished with the finest salt crystals from the Bitter Sea for just those occasions. It was just how things were, and a part of growing up in the Hollow of Snarth.

I was all too proud of myself, of course, for outdoing my big brother in these physical feats. More than once I teased Clay for being the smaller, weaker brother, in the way that fledglings tend to do. My parents, however, were seriously concerned with Clay's performance. "Clay should be doing better already, just look at Cleve," I heard them whisper to each other once. Only when we were fully fledged did I realize how hard it must have been on Clay.

One thing Clay always excelled at was academics. He devoured books on any subject in a matter of days and then could explain all their theories without missing a wing beat. He used to disappear into some secret place for nights at a time. It was moons before I realized he was off reading something that he just couldn't put down. Otulissa reminds me a lot of him in that respect. He was also quite good at the arts. No one in our family appreciated music the way he did. Da and Mum thought this was all very well and good, but they thought Clay needed more brawn to balance out his brains. "Still prefers his songs over his sword," Da would say, more than a little disappointed.

I, on the other wing, was all brawn, not a thought in my head. Clay would call me "WPB" sometimes — short for "wet pooper brains." I don't want to sound boastful, but I was the strongest flier that Firthmore had seen in generations — was navigating the katabats within a moon cycle of my First Flight. Dare I say, I was the Ruby of the Great North Waters? Well, I might be exaggerating there, but I was good.

So there we were, the two imperfect princes from the Hollow of Snarth. I overhead Mum say once that if she could just combine us into one owl, she'd have the perfect son. She meant well, I guess. I did learn later precisely why she wanted a "perfect son." It was a bit more complicated than you might think.

One night, Clay and I were sharing a nice fat mouse in our hollow. I remember it so vividly because it was a hard-won mouse. You know, when you're on the hunt for what seems like all night, and the little creature seems forever to be a talon-grab away. At the end of it, Clay was so ravenous that he almost butted my head going after the last bit of meat. He apologized for his uncouth behavior, and explained that he was starving because Da had made him do extra ice dagger drills earlier, and wouldn't let him eat until he could double his speed or power or something.

"I can't take it anymore, Cleve," he told me after we finished the mouse. "I don't know why Da is doing this to me. I hate it!"

I was about to launch into a good old-fashioned brotherly ribbing when Old Pan started mumbling something peculiar.

Old Pan, short for Pandorissa, was a Spotted Owl who had been in our family for generations. She was so old she was my grandda's nursemaid. Some said, jokingly of course, that she was so old that she knew Hoole himself. Nobody knew her age, but we were sure there was none older in all of the firths. Old Pan was no longer a nursemaid for my family. We all figured that our family kept her around because she had nowhere to go. She would do the occasional tidying of the hollow and such, but mostly, she entertained the chicks with her stories. I first heard the legends spoken from her very beak.

As I was saying, Old Pan mumbled something peculiar as Clay and I finished tweener. I didn't even know what it was at the time, but now I know it was "*Iso Veikko tahto olla prinssi joka on lupaus.*"

The strangest thing was, she spoke not in Krakish, or in any dialect of Krakish I had ever heard of. It was a language so ancient and so obscure that it's considered dead. Clay and I knew nothing of dead languages back then, but Clay would later figure out that Old Pan had spoken in the language of the ancient Northern Prophecies, the language that the Glauxian Brothers call Kratean. It was never spoken anymore, only written.

Old Pan was old, but not old enough to have spoken Kratean. Nor was she a scholar who might have come across it in her studies. Besides, no one really knew what it was supposed to sound like, exactly. She kept repeating those words over and over before she waddled out of the hollow.

So there I was, thinking Old Pan was mumbling nonsense — I wouldn't have known Kratean from raven caws. But Clay paid close attention. He memorized what she said, and, just as you would, went to our very limited family library to try to figure it out.

His search led him to a scroll about our family history — the history of the Hollow of Snarth. Much of it was just a record of who married whom, who fought in which battle, whose chick was born when, that sort of stuff. But he also found in it bits of Kratean, interspersed through the records. He could not figure it out by himself, his tutors wouldn't have taught him such things. So he took the scroll to the trusty Glauxian Brothers at the retreat. He snuck away for two nights to go to the island in the Bitter Sea. I covered for him, of course. I didn't think he'd find anything important, but thought he should get away from the old hollow, and from Da and all his demands, for a bit.

When he returned, he flew into my hollow, puffed up his chest, looked me straight in the eyes, and said, "I best take up an ice sword and battle claws, it seems I must become a warrior."

"That's what you learned, Clay?" I joked. "Isn't that what Da has been telling you . . . oh, I don't know, your entire life?"

The look on Clay's face told me he thought it was no joking matter.

"I'm the big brother. I'm the Prince Who Is Promised," he said.

"The what who is what?" I teased.

Clay rolled his yellow eyes and laid down a scroll.

"Here, the 'Prince Who Is Promised.'" He pointed to a passage that I couldn't begin to read or understand. "According to the brothers, this says, 'In the age of strife and tyranny, a prince shall emerge, a prince promised to us by the stars themselves. This great warrior shall be a savior of saviors.'"

I could tell Clay was beside himself with excitement. His eyes always glowed a bright gold when he discovered something new and fascinating in one of his books or in a piece of music.

Then, he retrieved our family scroll. "And here, right after the record of our hatching, this says, 'The big brother shall be the Prince Who Is Promised. The prince who shall banish the fire of evil and save the light of wisdom . . .' or something like that."

"Or something like that?" I asked. I was quite dubious of all this, you see.

"There aren't exact translations for some of the words. Like, here." Clay pointed to a part of one line with his talon. "This word 'kiista,' it can either mean strife or illness. The brothers figured it was more likely to be strife. And this, this word could mean either wisdom or fruit."

"Or *fruit*. You're supposed to, let's see, save some fruit?" I was becoming more and more convinced that Clay had stumbled upon a lot of nonsense.

"Well, clearly wisdom would the better definition here. The Glauxian Brothers were quite intrigued by this, Cleve, don't make light of it! The Northern Prophecies have been revered for generations, and what we have here is an important document. And I, the big brother, am apparently quite important to the future of owlkind!"

"Listen to yourself, Clay!" I said with a churr. "A few days ago, you were complaining that Da was making you do too many drills. Now you're out to save owlkind as the Prince Who Is Promised? All because of Old Pan?"

"Yes. I must do this. These prophecies are important. Just such a prophecy foretold the coming of Hoole. Don't you believe in them?" he asked.

"Maybe. But this one came from Da's old nurse-maid, Clay."

Honestly, I was at a bit of a loss. I didn't know why I was arguing with him.

"Cleve," Clay continued, "even if you don't believe in the prophecy, even if you don't think I am the Prince Who Is Promised, what harm will it do if I prepare for the moment, just in case? Will you just help me to train? Like you said, isn't that what Da and Mum would want, prophecy or no?"

He had a point, of course. I didn't believe in this prophecy business, but I'd be doing good to help Clay train anyway.

"All right, big brother — Your Princeliness," I told him. "I guess there's no harm in believing. I'll help you with your warrior training. Da and Mum are going to be thrilled to pieces, you realize."

The very next night, Clay began training like he was some sort of hero owl from the legends. He really dove into it, beak and claw. Master Benard, the old master-at-arms, was astounded. Da was outright shocked — happy, but shocked. Where Clay used to be timid around weapons, he became more daring. His began to fly farther and into stronger winds. He became very interested in warcraft, studying it and researching it with the intensity he previously had only for music. He grew stronger in wing and talon.

For a while, it all seemed to be going very well for Clay. I was proud of him. My big brother was finally starting to live up to my family's expectations, and he seemed to be pleased. Only . . . his approach always seemed a bit academic. His head was in it, for sure, but he lacked that certain . . . oh, how should I put it — gizzardly instinct.

I've always believed it's something you can't teach an owl, it has to come from within the second quadrant of the gizzard. Well, even if I couldn't teach it, I thought I could at least encourage it in Clay. I would go on to find the perfect opportunity to do so when winter came.

For several nights after our ice weapons practices, Clay and I would gleek about the armory, playing innocent pranks on Master Benard. When he took inventory of the weapons, Clay and I would hide a weapon while he was trying to keep count, and just when he'd think it was lost, we'd put it back in its place as if it had been there all along. Sometimes, we would replace one weapon with another, and he would think he was seeing things. It drove him crazy! Benard had a tough exterior, but inside, he was warm and jovial. We knew he might find our pranks mildly annoying, but we also knew he could take a joke.

One night, Clay and I went into the armory with Master Benard. We had just had to cut short our battle claw drills as a fierce blizzard was threatening. We were on our way to return our practice claws. As we went past the display area for the Mountain Claws, Benard did a double take. He went toward the wall to take a closer look. All of sudden, his voice rang out with fury.

"Claymore! Cleve! You've gone too far this time! It's one thing to have a lark with an ice scimitar, it's quite another to mess with one of the clan heirlooms. The two of you know better than to play games with it. What would your father say? Now, produce the Mountain Claws this instant!"

We had no idea what he was yelling about. We went in for a closer look. That's when we saw that the battle claws hung on the display hook were *not* the Mountain

Claws, but a pair of common battle claws polished to look like the ancient weapon. Clay and I were dumbfounded. We hadn't moved the claws, hadn't touched them at all. We were innocent! We would never play games with the family heirlooms; we knew better than that. Clay and I spoke out at the same time, proclaiming our innocence. The shocked looks on our faces must have told Master Benard that we were telling the truth.

It seemed that in the same instant, Master Benard, Clay, and I all arrived at the same conclusion.

Master Benard called for Jak. There was no answer. He called again, the suspicion building in his voice, and in our minds. He called a third time. By then, we knew there would be no answer. We went looking for him. Clay and I knew that he often liked to take short naps in the library, so we looked there. Master Benard looked in the dining hollow, where Jak would sometimes pilfer snacks. There was no sign of him.

Jak was gone, and so was our most precious family heirloom. Da was notified at once. There was quite a commotion, as you can imagine. Amid the hubbub, Clay nudged me. Then, he headed toward the back of the armory, where the ice weapons are kept, and signaled for me to follow. As we walked through the increasingly narrow passageway, Clay told me a secret.

"I know something about this armory that I think few other owls do," he began. "Remember when I used to disappear to read my books as an owlet? This is where I came."

"Here?" I asked. "Why here? And how did no one see you? This place is always bustling."

"Well, not in *that* part of the armory," he nodded toward the main room, where Da and Master Benard were still talking. "When I was really small, when I first started branching, I discovered, by accident, an old back entrance to the armory. I had stumbled on a branch, and almost smacked right into the trunk of the tree. I didn't hit solid trunk as I thought I would, but instead I fell through a patch of lichen into a small hollow. At least I thought it was a small hollow. . . ."

We kept walking and as Clay spoke, the passage sloped downward. It was getting so narrow that we had to duck our heads to get through.

Clay continued, his voice barely above a whisper. "I became curious and started to venture into my new-found hollow. I walked and walked, but it seemed never ending. Finally, I squeezed through a tiny hole, and I was in the back of the armory. I had found a hidden back entrance! Or perhaps it was just forgotten because it was so narrow."

Clay stopped. He turned to me and his voice grew serious. "The winds are fierce. I have a feeling that Jak has not been able to get away with the Mountain Claws yet. I think he's still here."

"You think Jak knew about this back entrance, then?" I asked.

"Jak spends more time in the armory than any owl, even more than Master Benard. He has nothing to do but polish one pair of battle claws. Don't you think he would have wandered back here one day and discovered the entrance?"

"You have a point there," I answered. "But why wouldn't he have already taken off with the battle claws?"

"Think, WPB! We were in the armory at tween time, and they were still on the display hooks, I'm sure of it. Since then, the only opportunity he had to replace the Mountain Claws with the dummy claws was while we were out doing drills. The winds were already so fierce that it was tossing us about like owlets. There is no way an owl who is unaccustomed to flying with battle claws could have flown far in this weather. And what better hiding place than this passage, where he could snatch them from the back entrance and leave without anyone noticing?"

Clay made perfect sense. But I wouldn't be convinced that the Mountain Claws would be found there until I saw them with my own eyes. Sure enough, I did.

"Jak! Halt!" Clay called out as we got to the end of the narrow passage. I was stuck directly behind my brother and could barely see into the entryway. I craned my head around Clay's just in time to see Jak standing at the edge of hollow. He turned toward us, the Mountain Claws strapped to his talons.

"Master Claymore! Master Cleve!" Jak called out in a panic. "Please . . . please don't come any closer!"

That owl was a wreck. I saw now that the blizzard was upon us with all its power. The winds howled just outside the hollow, and the snow made it impossible to see beyond more than your wingspan. Jak must have tried to fly away, but was blown back. His feathers were bedraggled, and he looked like he was scared for his life.

"Give us back the battle claws, Jak. We don't want to hurt you," Clay said calmly.

I, on the other wing, could not contain my anger. "How dare you, you worthless thief! Do you realize whom you're stealing from?"

"I'm sorry. I'm very sorry, Master Cleve. But . . . but I have no choice," Jak said.

"What do you mean, Jak?" When Jak didn't answer, Clay continued, "Of course you have a choice, you can choose not to take that which is not yours."

I wanted to lunge at that simpleton, but Clay barred my way.

"Master Claymore, I have no choice. Those other owls, they said they would hurt my sister if I didn't bring them these battle claws."

"What other owls?" Clay asked, more patiently than I had the gizzard for.

"The owls from the Hollow of Kyran," Jak answered. "They said these claws belonged with them other ones."

"The Hollow of Kyran? Our cousins?" I asked, baffled.

Clay was surprised as well, but he understood. "You mean our cousins on the other side of Firthmore? The ones who own Unguis Oceania?"

"Yes, sir," Jak replied, "them other ones." He lifted a foot to indicate that he was talking about the other pair of ancient battle claws from the Clan of Krakor. Jak went on, "They said that these battle claws belong to them. That the two pairs should never have been separated. And that I had to bring these back to their rightful owners."

"This is absurd!" I said. "We are the rightful owners of the Mountain Claws! They have been in the Hollow of Snarth for generations! This is thievery, plain and simple. Now give them back!"

"Please, they said they would hurt my sister if I didn't bring these to them before the new moon. They got her! I have to!"

"Jak, we will help you get your sister back. Just give back the battle claws and come into the hollow. We'll talk about this with Da and Master Benard. They'll forgive you and help you, I'm sure of it," Clay consoled.

But it was no use; Jak turned toward the entrance and lifted off into the blizzard. I rushed at him, forcing Clay forward and out of the hollow ahead of me.

The two of us burst out of the hollow after Jak. Clay and I were being tossed around by the fierce winds. I could barely make out Jak, just a few wing beats away, struggling to fly. I flapped my wings harder, determined to catch the thief. Being the stronger flier, I was on top of Jak within a moment.

I looked for Clay. Just as I turned my head, I saw the gleam of the Mountain Claws a feather's width from my eye; Jak was within reach. My talons swiped at the air, grasping for the young squire, while I used all my strength to keep my wings beating.

"Cleve, look out!" I heard Clay shout.

I saw Clay out of the corner of my eye, a few wing-spans away, struggling against the gale.

The next thing I knew, Jak was on top of me, flailing madly. I don't know if he was trying to use the Mountain Claws or if he was simply flailing, but he came toward me, claws first. I felt a sharp pain in my port wing. I lashed out blindly, with the might of an owl fighting for his life.

"Clay, help! I'm hurt!" I called out, barely staying aloft.

Suddenly, I was hit by a mass of feathers, claws, and beaks. I began tumbling out of the sky. It was chaos. The howling of the wind made it impossible to tell who was shouting. Was it Clay? Jak? Or maybe it was me. The swirling snow made it impossible to see. I flapped my injured wing as hard as I could, and managed to pull out of the free fall.

Clay and Jak were not so lucky. I watched as they hit the ground.

I landed as quickly as I could. The winds were still fierce, but manageable closer to the ground. I was horror-struck by what I saw. The two owls, my brother and our squire, lay there, lifeless. Jak had been dashed against rock in his fall. Clay must have fallen on top of him. He was stabbed through the chest by the Mountain Claws.

Clay had wanted to avoid violence and reason with Jak, but I rushed in, talons first, in my pursuit of clan honor. He was trying to help me. I lost my brother that night, and my clan lost its prince. He was killed in a pointless, unintentional skirmish, stabbed through by the very battle claws he was to inherit.

From that moment on, I forswore all use of weapons, all violence, all war. I vowed to never fight again.

As for Jak's sister, my family was able to find her and free her from her captors. Da, Master Benard, and I went to the Hollow of Kyran to speak with our cousins. It turned out that the kidnapping was the doing of one mad owl who was a new mate to one of our cousins. He had terrible delusions about his own importance to the royal history of the Clan of Krakor, and sought to reunite Unguis Montania with Unguis Oceania. He thought that if he possessed both pairs of ancient battle claws, he would somehow rule over both the Hollow of Kyran and the Hollow of Snarth. He had kidnapped Jak's sister without our cousins' knowledge, and certainly without their approval. He was cast out of the hollow when the truth was revealed.

After Clay's Final ceremony, I went to the island in the Bitter Sea for some peace. I discovered that reading and studying brought me the serenity I sought. I still miss Claymore dearly. It was for him that I took up the art of healing. I began healing others to heal myself.

It has always been hard for me to talk about what happened, but it feels good to get it out of my gizzard. Claymore deserves to have his story told. Now, after all this time, you know why I am a pacifist.

Dear Reader, allow me to add a final thought.

Cleve believed that the prophecy spoken by Old Pan was utter nonsense. I don't blame him, given what happened, but I'm not so sure that the prophecy was false.

Old Pan had said that the Prince Who Is Promised would be a savior of saviors in a time of strife and tyranny, that the Prince would banish the fire of evil. It was the words "fire of evil" that first got me thinking. Those words immediately conjured the image of the Striga in my mind. Not long ago, the Striga, with the support of Nyra, had planned a most terrible hatching of hagsfiend eggs. Cleve and I discovered this plot and brought information about the Striga's and Nyra's doings back to the great tree and to all the good owls of the world. During our reconnaissance

177

mission, we were attacked by fiendish blue owls who were at the command of the Striga. Had Cleve not been there and used the way of Danyar to defeat those blue owls, I would have certainly perished.

Is it not possible, then, that Cleve is the Prince Who Is Promised? Both he and his brother believed that the prophecy referred to Claymore — the older brother. But he admitted that Kratean, the language that the prophecy was written in, could not be easily translated. I think when Old Pan said "the big brother shall be the Prince Who Is Promised," she meant "big," as in "large," not "elder." If that was the case, the prophecy was certainly referring to Cleve, the larger owl of the two.

Cleve saved me. Without his heroic act, the forces of good may not have prevailed in the War of the Ember. Oh, it boggles the mind and rattles the gizzard. If Cleve hadn't lost his brother, he wouldn't have chosen pacifism. If he hadn't become a gizzard-resister, he wouldn't have learned the way of Danyar. How strange and astounding it is that the prophecy was fulfilled in the end. He will always be my prince.

Afterword:
Otulissa's Farewell

There you have it, Dear Readers.

I am sure there are many other tales of valor as yet untold in the hollows of this venerable tree. Someday I may collect them into another volume like this one. Perhaps you carry such tales of your own, but are not ready to open the book of your heart to others. Or maybe you are young and your adventures lie ahead.

However, for the near future I shall put aside my quill, because I, Otulissa, historian and ryb, have new duties awaiting my attention: a clutch of eggs! In less than three moon cycles from the printing of these tales, Cleve and I will be busy with the care of four owlets. It is my greatest hope that from me they will learn the fierce arts of war and the history of the Great Ga'Hoole Tree, and from Cleve, the healing arts and the history of the Northern Kingdoms. Then each will grow according to their nature, and become Guardians in their turn, ready to preserve the tradition of nobility and learning at the great tree, and to protect it, if necessary.

But there is news more important than mine, something astonishing and unprecedented: The Great Ga'Hoole Tree is itself setting seed! At the very top of the tree where the sun touches its uppermost branches, a great golden flower has bloomed. Soren has named it the Flower of Peace, for it seems the peace we fought so long for has nourished it. And just below the flower, a seedpod swells. The parliament meets soon to discuss the future of the seed. As I write, wise and learned creatures of all kinds are traveling to join the parliament for this special session, for the prospect of another great tree such as ours concerns all good creatures everywhere.

I can leave you with no better news than this: The Great Ga'Hoole Tree thrives. May you likewise be well and keep goodness and nobility of thought and deed alive in your gizzards!

Yours ever,

Otulissa

Northern Kingdoms

Glauxian Brothers'
Retreat

Bitter
Sea

Kiel Bay

Stormfast Island

Bay of Fangs

Everwinter Sea

Ice Talons

Ice
Narrows

Dark Fowl Island

Southern
Kingdoms

Beyond the Beyond

Shadow Forest

Silvervei

Southern
Kingdoms

The Barren

Forest
Kingdom
of
Ambala

St. Aegolius Canyons

St. Aegolius Academy
for Orphaned Owls

N